The Watchers

By Alan Peck

Published by Alan Peck Publishing in conjunction with Amazon Kindle Direct Publishing.

Copyright © Alan Peck   July, 2020

ISBN 979-8664333848

Acknowledgements

I need to thank a number of people who have helped me with this book. Firstly, my lovely wife Olive for her patience, feedback and proof reading. I have written this during the COVID-19 lockdown and it has been a wonderful escape from decorating, gardening and household chores. Olly has given me the quiet time I needed to get on and write.

Thanks are also due to Denise, Paul, Ian, Jenny, Helen and Rick who have given me invaluable feedback and helped to spot my many typos.

I was particularly grateful to Julian Milsom – the Station Manager for Felixstowe Coastwatch. It was very important to me that I had his backing for a story which is so obviously based on the whole idea of Coastwatch. Julian's positive review and support was much appreciated.

Finally, any remaining errors are entirely my fault and my responsibility.

Chapter 1

It was to be an ill-fated maiden voyage for the Ocean Traveller. Not on the Titanic scale, but still one that would end in death and much deliberation over exactly what happened and how on earth it could have happened.

She was a brand new 'ultra large' container ship on her maiden voyage from Shanghai to Felixstowe via Rotterdam. At four hundred metres long she was as big as anything in the container world. A new vessel under the command of a new captain who was getting to know his new crew.

It had left Shanghai with a cargo of 14,279 containers – some twenty-foot long and some forty-foot. Shanghai is the biggest container port in the world and Rotterdam the biggest in Europe. Felixstowe is merely the biggest in the UK. With a draft of 15.2 metres it only had a few feet of clearance at low tide to the sea bed of the deep-water channel approach to Felixstowe. Having unloaded 4,896 boxes in Rotterdam and taken on 2,117 it was still pretty full and sitting low in the water.

The hold was stacked with containers ten deep and the main deck was piled high with more - ten high and twenty-five wide across the full beam of the ship. The drive to pack ever more boxes into the new generation of ships meant the designs were ever changing. Gone was the traditional gently curving hull design, replaced by hulls which were almost rectangular for most of the length of the ship. Manoeuvrability was sacrificed for capacity.

Captain James Kirkwood took his early morning stroll around the decks, looking for lashings that had come adrift, visible leaks from boxes and sniffing for noxious fumes. His route was the best part of a mile and then he took the lift nine decks up to the Captain's deck, where his suite of rooms were. The newness of the vessel meant that the all-pervasive smell of heavy diesel oil he had been used to on all his previous ships wasn't yet noticeable.

With its gym, library, cinema and spacious accommodation it was a far cry from what he had been familiar with. The crew only totalled twenty-four but the state-of-the-art technology meant that was just about enough. The officers came from all over the world but the rest of the crew was entirely Filipino – the cheap but reliable sea-going labour found throughout the industry.

The voyage from Shanghai had been largely free of incident although there were various glitches with some of the electronic equipment That should have all been sorted during sea trials but it wasn't. He knew it was simply inevitable in today's hi-tech world. At least there had been no major mechanical problems and the huge engines had powered her reliably along at twenty-three knots.

When he sat in his chair on the bridge he was almost fifty metres above sea level but the huge mountain of boxes meant he couldn't see anything for half a mile dead ahead of the bows.

The pilot had boarded the ship some ten miles out from Felixstowe, to guide Ocean Traveller along the zig-zag route of the deep-water channel. Two tugs – Newlyn and Exmouth – were waiting just outside of the estuary, ready to turn her on the last leg of her journey to the new Number 9 deep-water terminal on the seaward end of Felixstowe port. Six of the biggest cranes in the world, costing twenty-five million pounds each, were waiting to do the unloading.

The tugs were nearly as new as Ocean Traveller – built in Vietnam to an impressive specification that enabled them to turn on the proverbial sixpence and exert up to sixty tons of pulling power. The crew that delivered Exmouth from the far east had been mighty pleased with it's manoeuvrability when pirates had attempted to board her. The skipper put one engine full ahead and the other full astern and spun it on the spot while turning the powerful water cannon on the pirate's boat. It was unlikely they would ever attempt to take a tug again.

As the three vessels entered the estuary of the River Orwell, Harwich was to their left and Felixstowe docks to their right. With only just over a mile to go the tugs both had a line attached to the Ocean Traveller and the two skippers both dialled in fifty tons of pull on the winch's digital displays. They were both lying astern, Exmouth on the port quarter and Newlyn to starboard. As the lines came taut they started to swing the stern of Ocean Traveller around as they lined it up for the final approach.

Both of the tug skippers and the captain and pilot on board Ocean Traveller had previously noted just two craft ahead of them on the starboard bow – both yachts. They were similar - Bermuda rigged sloops, white hulls and about thirty feet long.

Both were on the edge of the deep-water channel – almost abreast of each other – they looked as if they wanted to cross to the south. The rule was they should use the designated crossing point and keep well out of the way of any large vessel.

The public viewing point and café was situated right next to Number 9 terminal, where the Ocean Traveller was headed. The local paper had carried a piece about the maiden voyage of another huge visitor to their port. Many of them would have checked the Felixstowe Port website to check its ETA. The car park and café were both full with ship spotters eager to see another huge new arrival. They had absolutely no view of her yet but she would soon be appearing to their left.

There were a few walkers on the nature reserve at Landguard Point – the entrance to the estuary and adjacent to the final turning point in the deep-water channel. They would have had the best view of anyone but they were either studying the bird life or playing with their phones.

Tommy Carlton, skipper of Exmouth, radioed his counterpart Jason Kirk on board the Newlyn.

'Those bloody yachts are chancing their arm. Looks like they can't wait to cross the channel but they'll have to hang on until we're past.'

Jason replied. 'Yeah, stupid sods. Probably want to get close up pics of the new ship on their phones. They both need to turn to port pretty damn soon.'

Both tugs were now on the Ocean Traveller's port quarter as they strained to pull the stern over to the Harwich side of the estuary. The ship was now obscuring their view of the two yachts. Captain Kirkwood had seen the yachts from the bridge wing and turned to the pilot.

'Do you normally get yachts chancing their arm like those two?'

'Oh usually they're quite good but these two aren't - I'll be reporting them once we get alongside. Nothing we can do – it's up to them to keep out of our way.'

The captain turned to his second officer. 'Sound five short blasts.' Officially this meant 'I do not understand your intentions'. Unofficially it meant 'What the bloody hell are you doing you bozos?'

The radar system was now emitting a loud beeping noise as it sensed vessels dangerously close to the ship's path.

Once the Ocean Traveller was straightened up and pointing towards it's berth the Newlyn came around the stern and had a clear view ahead and to starboard. Jason got on the radio to Tommy.

'Hey, can you see one of those yachts to port? I can only see one to starboard. The other stupid sod must have cut across the bows of Ocean Traveller at the last minute.'

'No, there's nothing to port Jason.'

'So where the hell did he go?'

At that moment the radios came to life with Dover Coastguard tasking the Harwich RNLI station to send lifeboats out to attend a collision that had just taken place between Ocean Traveller and an unidentified yacht. Under the new Coastguard structure the 'super centre' at Dover was responsible for the whole coastline all the way up to the River Deben, just north of Felixstowe.

Tommy was back on the radio. 'Somebody has obviously seen what happened – probably Coastwatch or Seawatch. Nobody else would have got on to Dover that quick.'

It eventually transpired that a total of only five people had seen the collision - one was dead and the others didn't agree over just what happened.

Chapter 2

Jim Ellis gazed out of the lookout windows on to a typically quiet morning. There was the usual smattering of small craft – a few yachts, two fishing boats, the Harwich pilot boat and one lone kayaker paddling aimlessly around. A tug poked its nose out of the estuary - ready to usher another container ship full of goodies from China on to the Felixstowe dockside.

It was a pleasant spring morning with glimpses of the sun and enough of a breeze to tempt a few yachties out for maybe their first outing of the new season. After a winter of tedious hull scraping, painting and all the usual chores associated with boat ownership, people were eager to actually get out on the water.

To the left he could see the busy seafront, stretching past the amusements, fish and chip shops and ice cream stalls down to the pier. To the right he could see the nature reserve, leading to Landguard Point, the estuary of the River Orwell and the giant flamingo-like cranes of Felixstowe docks.

There were three distinct parts to the Felixstowe coastline. To the north the golf course led to Felixstowe Ferry at the mouth of the River Deben. The ferry was actually a small motor-boat which took people across the Deben on demand to the little hamlet of Bawdsey. The area was populated by a hotch-potch of boatyard sheds, a pub, two cafes, a wet fish shop and disparate dwellings which looked fortunate to have ever gained planning permission.

The main seafront area had the pier as its focal point with all the usual assortment of children's amusements, food and drink stalls and typical seaside tat. It was still a pleasant walk with lots of little bays created between the rock groynes and an assortment of brightly painted beach huts. The groynes had been much criticised when the rocks had first started to arrive on ships from Scandinavia but through the years they had won most people over. The bays were ever-changing, sometimes sandy, sometimes pebbly and often a mix of the two. Often Jim would pick the most sandy one and log it in his memory ready for his next swim, only to find that a month later it was all stones and he needed to seek out an alternative.

To the south the nature reserve was incongruously situated between the sea and the docks. Jim liked the contrast between the heathland with its variety of birdlife and rabbits and the busy dock area. The deep-water channel enabled the biggest container ships in the world to berth next to the viewing area.

The walkers, and those just wanting some peace, tended to alternate between the ferry end and the reserve. Families and visitors unfamiliar with the town mostly headed for the pier area, which Jim's wife Sally snootily referred to as the fish and chip eater's paradise.

Jim was pleased he no longer owned a boat. He had been an enthusiastic weekend sailor but had tired of the hassle that went with boat ownership. It wasn't the cost – he wasn't short of money. The old adage of yacht ownership being akin to ripping up £20 notes while standing under a cold shower had a lot of truth to it, but that wasn't what turned him off. Now that he was retired and in his mid-60s he enjoyed the fact that he and Sally could do whatever they wanted without acquiring any new ties or responsibilities.

Sometimes they rented a cottage, sometimes they flew off for a city hotel break, sometimes they went on driving holidays across Europe or the US. All things which required just a little effort to make the bookings but with none of the ongoing responsibilities and maintenance concerns of a second home or a caravan or a motorhome. Despite his love of the sea they had no desire to go on a cruise – the huge floating palaces, with thousands of passengers stuffing themselves with food all day, held no attraction for them. Whenever he was on watch and sighted a cruise liner coming into Harwich he thanked his lucky stars he wasn't on it.

Felixstowe suited Jim, and Sally had grown to like it too. After all those years of commuting on the Bakerloo line, from Stanmore to the City, Felixstowe was literally a breath of fresh air. A pleasant little seaside town with just enough places to shop, eat and drink. Some people decried it for its big industrial dock area but to Jim that just made it more interesting. It was an unpretentious place, honest but certainly not posh.

They had looked at houses in the more upmarket and snootier towns of Aldeburgh and Southwold towards the north but their seascapes were often bleak with few if any craft visible from the shore. Felixstowe felt more alive with ships and boats of all sizes and types constantly on the move.

Moving from the London area meant that with the proceeds of a comfortable detached house and selling his stake in the accountancy firm he could afford a luxurious seafront property overlooking Felixstowe golf club. For the cost of an apartment in

Knightsbridge he had acquired a six bedroom, three bathroom house with a large balcony to the front and a secluded pool to the rear. He mused that Sally might have preferred the West End with its access to theatres, smart restaurants and expensive shops but that held no appeal for Jim.

He had done well for himself – actually, maybe just a teensy bit too well. He had played a major part in building the firm but he had also had a stroke of good fortune which he had to keep to himself. He thought about it every day of his life – there was no escaping it. It was the feeling you get when you run a red light – you tell yourself it had only just changed from amber, other drivers often crossed a second or two after the red, you were only doing what lots of people do – but deep down you know you ran a red light and you shouldn't have. Hopefully no busybody with a dashcam would shop you.

Lots of people indulge in some creative accounting from time to time but when you are a chartered accountant you can take it to a more inventive level. You know how the system works – you can analyse P&L statements and balance sheets with an insight not afforded to ordinary mortals and carefully massage audit trails with labyrinthine twists and turns.

Jim had always loved numbers. He loved the solidity, the logic, the truthfulness. He was always destined to follow in his father's footsteps. He loved maths at school and left the LSE with a first in economics.

When he first qualified he was over the moon to land a place in the graduate intake scheme at one of the big five accountancy firms. He sank all his savings into the purchase of a new brown suit which he proudly wore on his first day at the London Bridge headquarters building. He never forgot the humiliation of that first day with people pointing him out and laughing. Nobody had ever told him that he was entering a world where brown suits were as inapplicable as a tee shirt and jeans. Dad funded the rapid acquisition of a grey suit and the brown job never saw the light of day again.

That was probably the nadir of his career and after that the only way was up. With a half decent brain on his shoulders and a prodigious work ethic he was on his way.

Sally didn't share many of his traits but with her appreciation of the artistic side of life they gelled – the attraction of opposites. Jim didn't want her to understand the financial aspects of their life and Sally didn't want to know anyway. So long as she could eat in good restaurants, endlessly shop for clothes and handbags she didn't need and drink coffee and wine with her many friends she was happy.

As befitted the image of a chartered accountant Jim had always been cautious. He worried about the overinflated house prices, the people tacking another 30K on to their already enormous mortgage for a new kitchen they didn't need. He looked at the many new reg cars on the roads knowing that 9 out of 10 of them were financed by big monthly lease payments for drivers who would probably never own them. He knew we were a country living beyond our means.

Following the 2008 financial crash he figured it was just a matter of time before the next disaster came along. Maybe it would be triggered by another personal borrowing crash like the sub-prime mortgage debacle. He worried that the arch buffoon Trump

15

would send the world spinning into a devastating trade war or a middle eastern apocalypse.

As a consequence he moved his personal money into safe but boring fixed term bonds with very little of it being subject to the vagaries of the world of stocks and shares. For years he feared he was over cautious and was losing out by not being braver.

Sally had never known what it was to struggle. A comfortable upbringing as the daughter of a Surrey stockbroker had sheltered her from the harsher side of life. Her parents hadn't been over-impressed by her second-class arts degree or her choice of career as a jobbing actress landing the occasional poorly paid role in provincial plays. They tolerated that and accepted she was never going to set the world on fire but mum and dad were grateful for small mercies – she was a lovely person and had never dabbled in drugs as far as they knew or become a single parent.

They did totally approve of Jim though. A respectable type who had obviously done well for himself, rising through the ranks of a sizable and well-established firm in the City. They had begun to despair of her ever getting wed. A series of imperfect relationships with a diverse range of mostly arty types had all come to nothing. Sally's dad played golf with Jim a couple of times and they got on well. Jim was diplomatic enough to praise the good shots and sympathise with the many wayward ones.

He had joined Seawatch in an effort to get himself involved in the local community and make some new friends. They were a collection of mostly retired people with some sort of interest in the sea. Everyone was a volunteer and their role was to keep an eye out for anyone on the water or on the beach who might get into trouble. They used binoculars, radar, computers and a

CCTV system to oversee the waters from the River Deben, which led to Woodbridge, the Felixstowe area and the approaches to Harwich.

When Jim first volunteered, one of the old stagers told him that mostly nothing happened but that there was always the possibility of something enormous happening. He could see that plainly enough – the prospect of a big ferry colliding with a gigantic container ship was always present. In practice most of the incidents were much tamer – yachts running aground on the sandbanks at the Deben entrance and people falling out of kayaks and being unable to get back in.

He liked the vast majority of his fellow watchkeepers with their differing backgrounds and interests. Some were ex-servicemen, many had owned a boat of some description and some had no previous experience of the sea but a desire to learn and get involved. There were a few know-alls, keen to impress others with their superior knowledge, but mostly they were good company. Although most of the watchkeepers were men there were also a few ladies who were just as capable. Their presence helped the guys to keep their language clean and to at least make an effort to keep the kitchen and toilet areas fit for human habitation.

The tug had sidled up to the stern of the container ship, put a line across and was pulling the stern of it round towards the Harwich side of the estuary, ready to turn it before it berthed at Felixstowe docks. The kayaker was joined by two others and a lone paddleboarder. He looked through the binoculars to check that each of them were wearing some sort of buoyancy aid. He wondered idly whether paddle-boarding was as boring as it looked or whether he had missed some nuance that made it slightly interesting.

There were two small fishing boats near the Wadgate Ledge beacon to the south-east of the lookout. This used to be a favoured spot for fisherman but now they moaned about the lack of fish in that area. Jim had quizzed one of them about where all the fish had gone. He said his theory was that they had moved to the wind farms, which had effectively created artificial reefs they could feed on.

There were a couple of hardy souls rod fishing from the beach but Jim wondered how much fun that was as it was so rare to see them catch anything. He mused that it was different strokes for different folks and if it kept them happy then that was okay.

Jim went into the functional little bathroom at the back of the lookout. He used the loo, washed his hands and looked at himself sideways in the mirror to check his paunch. He knew he should lose a few pounds but he thought that for an old boy he didn't look too bad. He still had most of his mop of blonde hair – it was going a bit grey in places and he probably needed a haircut. When he took Sally coffee in bed first thing in the morning she usually responded with 'thanks Boris'. He knew there was a bit of a resemblance but tried to use a comb more frequently than the Prime Minister.

His fellow watchkeeper Steve Tomlinson put the kettle on and made them both a mug of coffee. He liked Steve – a retired dockworker – with a big jolly wife by the name of Trudy. Steve was always talking about Trudy's prodigious cooking. He claimed that when he went off for a day's fishing Trudy would use a whole loaf of bread for his sandwiches. Jim could believe that as he and Sally had sampled one of her famous roast beef Sunday lunches – it was a lovely meal but they both had difficulty walking for the rest of the day.

Steve had lots of tales to tell about his time in the docks. The containers that got lost and the freezer container full of meat that was shipped off to Canada three times because the paperwork wasn't right. Finally the entire contents had to be scrapped.

Apparently some 5,000 containers per year fall into the sea across the world due to a whole variety of bad weather and mishaps. Jim wondered how many were littering the seabed across the globe.

Steve often talked of the incredible meanness of the big shipping companies. Gigantic multi billion pound businesses who were forever working out how they could cut the crews to the bare bones on minimum rates of pay. He knew of one long standing captain who after a lifetime's exemplary service received an email from head office to tell him he would no longer be given a serviette with his meals. Instead he could have a sheet of kitchen roll and this would apparently save the company circa £25K a year across their huge fleet of ships.

The container ships were a sight to behold. Their vastness not apparent until you got up close and personal with them. Their capacity was measured in TEUs – twenty-foot equivalent units, relating to the original standard container size. These days most of the containers are forty-foot units. The biggest of these behemoths now had a capacity of some 24,000 TEUs and this was continually increasing as new hull and bridge designs allowed ever more to be crammed in. Jim tried to imagine one of those arriving fully laden and being wholly unloaded at

Felixstowe. If they all got transported onwards by lorry that would mean 12,000 trucks trundling up the A14.

Seeing all these huge ships coming and going gave Jim an insight to world trade. All those arriving from the far east were typically piled high with containers and sitting low in the water. All those leaving on the return journey usually had lots of empty space and were sitting high enough that you could see a large part of their rudder. Steve often said that a lot of containers on the outbound ships were either empty or full of rubbish for recycling in China.

When Jim first got into yachting he had taken some RYA courses to learn basic seamanship, reading a chart, plotting and using marine radios. This had helped when he joined Seawatch and had to prove that he could become a competent watchkeeper. He attended the monthly training sessions and diligently completed the test papers that were set.

After all the years of having to keep up to date with all the changes in the business world, and all the new software tools and techniques, Seawatch was a doddle. He still liked to have some ongoing learning and development to keep his old brain plodding along. Like many of his fellow watchkeepers he was aware that he was beginning to forget more and more as his short-term memory worsened.

Sally was beginning to get frustrated by the many little things he forgot at home. He would think of three things he needed from upstairs and would come down with just one of them. Last week he needed a wee when he was at the pub and discovered he had put his pants on back to front. He laughed at himself and regaled friends with the story but deep down it worried him a bit. Sally had started to refer to him as her doughnut boy.

Chapter 3

Saskia was running late. Her husband Colin had been up early and headed off to the marina for a day on his beloved boat. She had the day to herself and drifted off to sleep again.

The sun was peeking through the curtains and she mused that she didn't have to be anywhere until meeting Penny and Ruth at The Anchor for a girly lunch. Colin wouldn't be back until evening and would only want something quick and easy for dinner – probably a microwave meal, so no need for any prep.

She stretched, climbed off the bed and drew the curtains back. The sea was calm and she could see the Stena ferry on its way out of harbour en-route for the Hook of Holland, so she knew it must be getting on for 10'o'clock. There were a couple of yachts out already and a little cargo ship at anchor. The usual straggle of walkers were on the prom – some with dogs, some alone and a couple hand-in-hand.

She half liked their apartment but wished it were bigger. It was one of the larger ones on the top floor of a new development, set high up and just a hundred yards from the high-water line. The views were spectacular but when the wind really blew it was noisy and the carpets would lift slightly when there was an easterly gale.

Considering the price tag of £700,000 she didn't think much to the build quality and the resident's association were in a permanent battle with the developers. It was an awful lot to pay for a great sea-view. They had paid cash and hadn't bothered to have a full independent survey done. She ruefully reflected that if they'd had to get a mortgage they would probably have got some better independent advice on the valuation and potential leasehold problems. But what's done is done.

They had three bedrooms, two bathrooms and on the seaward side a large lounge area with a balcony that ran the full length of the room. The dining room was used by both of them as a study, as they ate all their meals in the kitchen/diner.

They had moved to Felixstowe from Cambridge when both of them opted for early retirement. The choice of dwelling had been a battle – she wanted a sizable detached house in a nice area, with a big garden. Colin didn't want to spend that much as his main desire was a boat. Eventually he persuaded Saskia that she would love a boat too. He smooth-talked her with visions of idyllic trips along the rivers Orwell and Stour and venturing out to sea when the weather was right.

He took her to the boat show in Southampton and she was sucked in by the gorgeous craft boasting luxurious accommodation and the promise of halcyon days to come. The reality was somewhat different when they examined the price tags and totted up all the costs of owning even a small yacht. It wasn't just the purchase price but the ongoing costs of moorings, boat yard maintenance, equipment, fuel, insurance etc.

They trekked around Felixstowe looking at houses and boats and after many minor spats and a few full-on rows they eventually came to a slightly uneasy agreement. Saskia had been taken in by the thought of a luxurious top floor apartment and Colin was prepared to go along with that if he could just have his boat.

Saskia secretly felt the apartment was nice but she knew it had been a bad investment. Soon after they moved in The Times had produced an expose' on the company who had developed the block and many more like it around the country. Her heart sank as she read that they had a track record of selling units at inflated prices to buyers who subsequently sold them at a loss. The developer had a reputation for high annual fees to cover all the general services like ground rent, window cleaning, maintenance, gardening and security etc.

There was no limit to the annual increases they could get away with levying on their powerless leaseholders. Those who wanted out found they could only sell through an agent appointed by the developer and in age of soaring property prices people were getting screwed down to accepting a hefty loss. All in all she felt they had been stitched up and there was no easy way out.

Saskia had hidden the article from Colin and hoped he wouldn't find out about it. She feared they would be stuck there forever and wished she had stuck out for the big detached house she had really wanted.

Colin had been far more enthusiastic looking at boats rather than houses. He had always been into boating but apart from a little cabin cruiser he went fishing in for a couple of years, he had never been an owner. He crewed for friends who had yachts and that had always been his dream.

He had eventually plumped for Tulip, a 33 foot Sun Odyssey – a sleek looking bermuda rigged sloop. It was five years old but looked like new and after a week of haggling he had eventually agreed a deal to buy it for a tad over £50,000. It had sails, an engine, two cabins and four berths. The little galley and bathroom were small but functional. Saskia had to admit she was impressed and they both daydreamed about sunny days, gentle cruises and boozy lunches.

The reality had of course been somewhat different. Yes, there had been warm sunny days when they had meandered along the river and anchored to enjoy a long lunch. There had also been days when they had ventured out to sea, Colin had hoisted the sails and Saskia had thrown up over the side. Even on what Colin said was a perfectly calm day with hardly enough breeze to fill the sails she had been ill. She was happy enough in the river but once past Felixstowe docks and out into the waves she hated it. Colin kept saying she should stick with it – she would get used to it and she would come to love the feel of being under sail. But she didn't – it didn't get any easier and she just equated the sea with illness. She knew Colin was disappointed but she couldn't help it.

They had settled into a routine of river cruising together on warm sunny days and doing their own thing when the weather wasn't smiling. Saskia would shop, visit friends and have long girly lunches while Colin either went to sea on his own or with a mate. He liked the solitude of being on his own but it was nice to have some labour available sometimes when the sails needed attention.

Saskia was born and raised in Cambridge by parents who were both academics. Dad was a maths lecturer at King's College and Mum was a research scientist for a drugs company on the

Science Park. It had always been taken as read that Saskia would follow in their footsteps so they were appalled when she took her A levels and, despite really good results, she absolutely refused to go to Uni.

She was hell bent on getting paid employment and becoming independent. No amount of parental cajoling, threats or bribery dissuaded her. She applied for an IT job in London with a big blue-chip computer manufacturer and was lucky that her lack of a degree didn't matter. The company recruitment process was firstly based on applicants sitting the IBM Programming Aptitude test. It didn't seem to matter whether she had two O levels or a first-class honours degree from Cambridge. The key factor was whether they thought she could code software which worked.

She sailed through the test and two interviews and was given an offer to work as a Trainee Programmer at a datacentre near Oxford Circus. She found a cheap bedsit in Peckham and began a new life of commuting on the tube every day.

From the first day she loved it. She had a natural affinity for programming, quickly made new friends and was thrilled to bits with her new life. Mum and Dad were scared stiff and thought she would be assaulted, made pregnant and become a druggie. But none of these things happened – she thrived and she was happy.

After her initial training she became an application programmer – writing code in Cobol. This meant writing code for run of the mill business applications. Before long she realised there was more money to be made as a systems programmer – maintaining and fixing the operating system software on huge corporate mainframe systems. Her salary package improved and after a couple of years and some help from the bank of Mum and Dad she had put down the deposit on a small flat in Islington.

Life changed again when the company offered her a new role evaluating software packages. The company had a catalogue of software packages which they had tested, approved and were prepared to recommend to their many corporate clients. Software companies were desperate to get their products into this catalogue as it virtually guaranteed big sales for them in return for hefty royalty payments.

Saskia was sent to head office in Sunnyvale, California – right in the heart of Silicon Valley for further training. She took to the new role like a duck to water. Having looked at the quality of the code, the documentation and the resilience of the software she then played the role of a typical customer using it for the first time. She figured that if she couldn't master almost all of what the software was supposed to do in half an hour then it was no good – the typical end-user customer wouldn't grasp it in a month of Sundays.

She quickly gained a reputation both within the company and across the many software developers who hoped their product would meet with her approval. She had become known as Sas to her colleagues and people talked about whether or not a product would be able to pass the Sas test.

By now Sas was regularly commuting between the London office and Sunnyvale. Travelling club class with BA she settled into a routine of flying to San Francisco, picking up a Hertz car and driving down Highway 101 to a 4-star Marriot in The Valley. Life was good and Sas was enjoying every minute of it.

Clients would wine and dine her hoping that would help to get their product approved. She enjoyed the meals and usually the company but was never sweet talked into anything. If the product failed the Sas test then it was 'thanks but no thanks'.

This was her life for many years with the company rewarding her with better salary packages, a Mercedes, bonuses and thank-you jaunts to various exotic places.

Things began to change when Tom was recruited to work under her wing. Tom was a pleasant enough lad with an MBA from Oxford and an amazing aptitude for any new technology. When teaching him how to do the product assessments she was alarmed to find he was getting to grips with new tech quicker than she was. This had never happened to Sas before – she had always outshone anyone she had worked with. Her confidence took a further blow when they took on a new graduate trainee. She phoned her Mum and said, 'Mum, I'm over the hill'. Mum laughed and said, 'I don't think so darling, whatever makes you think that?' Sas took a deep breath, 'Well I've taken on a new grad trainee and he's smarter than me – a spotty bloody graduate trainee, can you believe that?'

That was the beginning of a gradual acceptance that this was a youngster's game. She was starting to make notes about how to do stuff after years of telling people 'don't write stuff down – it's not necessary. Software is intuitive – just look at the bloody screen and figure out what to do next. If you write down click this and scroll down to that you are defeating the object – living in the stone age.' Now she was starting to do it herself and it was making her feel old.

Meeting Colin was a big turning point. He was also in IT but several years older than Sas, living in Cambridge where he worked for a networking business. He was an ex-programmer who had moved up into management. Instead of worrying about coding he now worried about spreadsheets – constantly looking at numbers and figuring out how he could get costs down and revenue up. His boss was in the US and whenever he spoke to him the first question was always, 'Are you making your numbers?' Never mind how are you, how is your love life, is it raining there again – always 'Are you making your numbers?'

The spreadsheets were like an ECG – showing up problems that, if not fixed, would likely be your demise. If the numbers were good then life was great – pats on the back, club class travel, more money and freebie trips to Hawaii. If the numbers were bad then life was rubbish – no bonus, travelling economy and getting beaten up by merciless inquisitors in the boardroom.

Colin's professional life was on a downward path, like Sas'. The old mainframe world that had been so dominant for so long was now in decline. Smaller, faster, distributed systems were the future. Like Sas he was aware that the youngsters could pick up the new tech so fast. When he changed his mobile for a new model it took longer and longer to get to grips with it. He thought more and more about how he could escape.

He met Sas at a launch party for some new product in the Science Park. She was expertly balancing a plate of nibbles and a glass of wine while making small talk. His first impression had been her shapely long legs. He had always been a leg man – a girl could have the best frontage in the world but he always checked out the legs first. She looked about fifty-ish, slim and wearing a classy looking flowery dress – shortish but appropriate and definitely not tarty. Her dark hair was cut short – business-like, but not severe.

They swapped the usual pleasantries about who they worked for and what they did and eventually he got her business card by promising to send her some marketing stuff he thought might be of interest. Sas saw straight through this ploy and smiled inwardly, but was happy to hand over her number and email address.

One thing led to another and soon they were dating. Sometimes they met in London, sometimes in Cambridge. A round of meals, the theatre, drinks. They really hit it off. Both were surprised to find out they were single and unattached – they laughed that a lifetime of travel and hard work hadn't left them enough time to think about marriage, kids and all the usual stuff. They often daydreamed about how life might be after IT. Early retirement was becoming an attractive prospect.

His proposal made her laugh – she said it was more like a business case then an offer of marriage. He outlined this rosy future of him selling his small house in Cambridge, Sas selling the Islington flat, both taking early retirement and retiring to the coast somewhere. However the more Sas thought about it the more sense it made and the more it appealed.

As a graduate of Kings Colin was keen to exercise his right to marry in the famous King's College chapel. Sas loved the idea and her parents were over the moon – happily funding all of the considerable cost.

The wedding was followed by some six months of negotiating early retirement deals with employers who didn't want them to leave and weekend trips to various coastal hotels as they searched for their ideal retirement location.

They flirted with the south coast and seriously considered the Brighton and Bournemouth areas but then made their first ever trip to Felixstowe. They both fell in love with the place. Sas looked online at lots of different houses and would have happily sunk most of their money into something spacious and upmarket. Colin wanted a smaller cheaper property, his boat and enough money left over that they could live really well with lots of holidays and eating out and no financial concerns.

Sas showered and put on a white blouse, jeans and blue denim jacket. She checked herself in the mirror and chuckled – thinking that for a retired old biddy she scrubbed up pretty well.

Penny and Ruth were already at the pub – chatting, giggling and getting stuck into a bottle of sauvignon blanc. They were the first new friends she'd made after moving to Felixstowe – meeting them at a do put on at Colin's yacht club. Ruth was a plump friendly type coming to grips with life on her own after losing her husband to cancer the year before.

Penny was a real laugh – flirty and outrageous. Despite being in her late sixties she would often make waiters blush as she complimented them on their sexy eyes or cute bums. Political correctness definitely wasn't her thing. Lunches with them were always long, boozy and enjoyable. They would all walk to the pub so there were no worries over just how many glasses of vino they had and they always split the bill three ways and left a generous tip.

It was nearly four'o'clock when they eventually said their goodbyes and Sas picked up a bit of grocery shopping on her walk home. Colin returned home a little later and she put his dinner in the microwave. He'd had a good day on his own – cruising along the Orwell using the engine and then once past Landguard Point he headed out to sea, hoisted the mainsail and pottered around for a couple of hours before heading back.

It was just about warm enough to sit out on the balcony. Colin tucked into his sweet and sour chicken, washed down with a beer. They both looked out to sea as they chatted about their day. There were more people on the prom now – walking off their dinners. Colin scanned the seascape with his binoculars – three small ships in the Cork anchorage, one really big container ship on the way out, one Dutch dredger on the way in and half a dozen small craft.

The forecast for the following day was good, more sun and less wind. They agreed it would be a good day for taking the boat up the Stour towards Manningtree. It would only take an hour and half to get there, they would anchor, lunch, doze and meander back late afternoon. They both thought that life really wasn't half bad.

Chapter 4

Sally was up early to make the bed and tidy up before Sue, the cleaner, arrived. Jim always said there was no point in having a cleaner if you were going to do it yourself but Sally didn't want Sue thinking she worked for a pair of slobs. She still had her dressing gown on and wouldn't get dressed until they'd had breakfast and Jim had gone out.

She put four slices of bread in the toaster and tipped bran flakes into two bowls, before adding a few chunks of tinned pineapple, some peach slices and a couple of prunes. The percolator was already brewing. Sally wondered if she should really be having two thick slices of toast with proper butter and marmalade every morning. She put the palm of her hand on her slight paunch and tried to figure if it was getting just a tiny bit too big. She had always struggled to keep her weight down but she liked to live comfortably.

Yesterday she had looked at a height/weight chart on the net which classified her as slightly overweight but a long way short of obese. She often thought that maybe she should drink a bit less wine, use low fat spreads and skip desserts occasionally but then she thought about the pleasure she got from living life as she liked. Maybe aiming to be just one stone above the recommended line was a perfectly acceptable compromise.

Jim was definitely on the tubby side but he was happy and never stepped on the scales. She was proud to be his wife and wanted him to be proud of her. He might warrant her pet name of Boris but she didn't want him to think of her as Mrs. Boris.

The toast popped up and she yelled to Jim that breakfast was ready. She knew it was a golf day for him and he appeared with a light green polo shirt tucked into fawn chinos. His hair hadn't seen a comb yet and the paunch protruding slightly over his belt warranted his nickname.

'Who are you playing with today?' she asked, more out of politeness than interest.

'Ronnie and Joe' he replied. 'We're playing stableford – a tenner each, winner takes all.'

'Are you having lunch in the clubhouse after?'

'Yeah, that's the plan – probably whatever the special is, with a couple of pints. What about you?' he asked.

She poured the coffee and put milk on their cereals. 'Oh I need to pick up some bits from Tesco and that new boutique opposite the cinema has got a really nice blue top and white trousers in the window. I might try them on. Then Margaret is coming over for a coffee after lunch and we're going for a walk along the coast path, past the ferry.'

They buttered their toast and heard the front door click as Sue let herself in. She appeared in the kitchen looking her usual scruffy self – jeans, tee shirt and her dark curly hair falling untidily to her shoulders. They both liked Sue – always cheerful, always

34

reliable and happy to turn her hand to anything. She had two children in primary school and dropped them off on her way to work.

Jim finished his breakfast, cleaned his teeth and headed to the garage to grab his golf bag and trolley. It was only a couple of hundred yards walk to the golf club.

Sally cleared the table and headed for the bathroom. She cleaned her teeth, showered and as she dried herself she looked in the full length mirror. As always her gaze lingered ruefully on her tummy and the slightly greying hair. She had been wondering about having a colour but thought it would look daft to go straight from greyish to blonde, or whatever. As always, she figured she was pretty much content with who she was.

She put on her light blue three quarter length trousers, a flowery blouse and a light cotton beige jacket. With loafers on her feet she checked herself in the mirror and decided she was ready for the day.

All through the years of theatre work Sally had given it her all – performing all over the country and always hoping the bit parts would grow into something more challenging and more rewarding. Mum and Dad had always been brilliant – helping out with money and always keeping her bedroom ready for whenever she needed it next. Even so she had stayed in some truly awful places – she often thought she should write a book on the dreadful B&Bs, hostels, friends spare rooms and doss houses she had lain her head in. In the early days Mum had often nagged her to get a proper job but eventually had given up and settled for her simply being the daughter that she was.

When the work started to dry up Sally decided to have a go at writing. She spent some six months at home writing what was essentially an autobiography – 'The Life of a Jobbing Actress'. She had been on a couple of creative writing courses and had a few short stories published in local magazines – without payment of course!

Mum and Dad and a couple of friends were willing proof readers and eventually she felt reasonably happy with the final draft. She bought the current edition of The Writers Yearbook and started contacting publishers. She sent off a covering letter, a synopsis of the book and the first two chapters. The response was totally demoralising – most publishers didn't reply, some sent her their standard rejection slip and one actually penned a note saying her work had some merit but sorry, they weren't interested.

She combed the net looking for further channels for writers and found one writer's forum that had a dismal piece stating that, of all the manuscripts sent to publishers, only an average of one in 400 would ultimately get into print.

After a couple of months of not doing anything much other than taking herself on long dismal walks through the woods, watching daytime TV and drinking way too much wine she decided that if nobody wanted it then she would bloody well publish it herself.

She studied online guides about how to do it and talked it through with her Dad. He was understanding and sympathetic but tried to tone down her expectations. 'Sal darling, I think it's really tough to produce and market your own book. Not for nothing do the book trade refer to it as vanity publishing.'

Sally looked at her feet – 'I know Dad but I'd get such a buzz to see a book with my name on the front and my picture on the back. I've got loads of contacts in the theatre world and with writers at trade magazines. I'm sure I could get the local media to give me some coverage – the local papers and radio stations are always short of material.'

Dad sighed – 'Have you thought how you would finance it? You'd have to use a professional copy editor and probably some sort of book production agent and then there's the physical printing costs.' Sally knew little about money and nothing about business. She looked downcast.

Her Dad smiled, 'Tell you what, do some more research, get all the steps figured out, pull together some quotes and amaze your old dad by producing a business case for him. You never know, if you make a good job of it you might possibly persuade him to give you a small business loan – at mates rates of course!'

Sally was thrilled and threw herself into it. After much time on the net and seeking multiple quotes from relevant suppliers, she used a business case template she found on a bank's website to pull it all together. She was horrified to find that when she added everything up she needed a minimum of £4,000 just to get a print run of 500 produced.

If she priced it at £6.99 and somehow managed to sell the lot she would still be making a loss. So she massaged the numbers – upped the jacket price a bit, went for a print run of 1,000 and convinced herself she could somehow sell them all, repay Dad and make a small profit.

Dad listened to her proposal intently, asked lots of questions, privately convinced himself she hadn't got a cat in hell's chance and said that okay, she could have the money. She was his daughter, he loved her and he couldn't stand the sort of wet spaniel look that would be on her face if he said no.

Of course, Dad's hunch was right and the book was a flop. Sally had her book reviewed in two trade magazines, was thrilled to see her picture in the local press and was interviewed by two local radio stations. She certainly worked hard enough but after a year she had sold exactly 580 copies and had over 400 stacked in boxes in a corner of her bedroom. Dad got a bit of money back but he'd always known it was a bad deal for him.

In fact Dad was a brick. Sally was now prepared to give up on a writing career – she was no more a talented writer than she was an actress. But one night Dad came back from the pub in a good mood and tapped on her bedroom door.

'Hi Dad – what's new with you then?'

'I've been talking to this guy in the pub – turns out he's a writer. We got chatting and I told him about your book.'

Sally raised her eyebrows, 'Oh God, I bet he was impressed'.

'Well, actually he was brutally honest. He said you were on a loser from the start. Everyone wants to write their autobiography and 99.9% are stunningly boring. He said if you write your life history it's only of interest to a handful of friends and relatives and you'd never make any money from it.'

'So what does he do if he's so smart? Does he make any money from writing?'

'Well, he says he does now, but he only started to when he used a completely different way to self-publish. Apparently Amazon have a set of software tools which anyone can use for free. They guide you through the process, help format your book, create a cover for you, give you an ISBN number and a barcode. He said he's no IT genius but he'd been able to figure out how to do it.'

Sally looked interested. 'So what's in it for Amazon?'

'Well they check out the finished article, publish it and market it for you on their website. When a customer buys it they print it on-demand and send it to the customer.'

Sally looked quizzical. 'Sounds too good to be true.'

Dad smiled – 'Well apparently Amazon have these incredible printing facilities – churning out thousands of different books of all different sizes as the orders roll in. The author pays them for the actual printing and they take a sizable cut to give themselves a decent profit. He says you don't need to pay for a whole load of books to be printed which you might never sell.'

He pointed to the pile of boxes in the corner. 'You wouldn't have all these and you wouldn't have to worry about distribution if and when you did get sales.'

Sally looked doubtful. 'So what does the author end up with – about 20p per book ?'

Dad grinned. 'This guy said his last book was a textbook – something to do with IT. He put a price of £14.99 on it and when all is said and done Amazon pay him £5.75 for every copy sold.

Sally's eyes were out on stalks. 'So he produces books for next to nothing – apart from the cost of his time – and gets over a fiver net for each one?'

'That's right. Of course you'd still have to think about what you could write that anyone would want to read.'

Sally gazed into space. 'Maybe I could have a go at fiction?'

Dad stood up. 'Maybe – well it's something to think about. Check it out on the net. This guy says there are people who've written upwards of twenty books this way and every month they get a nice fat payment credited to their bank account. All you need to figure out is what the hell you could write about.'

So to Dad's amazement she did the research , thought of an idea, got to grips with the software tools and published the first of what turned out to be a series of books featuring a private detective by the name of Jack Hubbard. Jack got involved in various mysterious cases relating to the theatrical world so she was able to draw on past experience.

The books didn't sell in huge numbers but she was able to eke out a meagre living which did a lot for her self-respect and delighted Mum and Dad.

It was through the book that she first met Jim. She had been flattered to be asked to give a talk on the Jack Hubbard series at the Orwell hotel, as part of the Felixstowe book festival. Jim was in the small audience, bought a copy of the latest book in the series and asked her to sign it. He had read all the previous five books and was keen to chat to her about them. With a small queue forming for signings he suggested buying her a drink in the bar later.

Over two glasses of wine they chatted and immediately hit it off. Sally was staying at the hotel for the weekend and they had dinner together the following evening. Before long Jim was visiting her at her parent's home near Guildford for weekends and then Sally got her first invitation to spend a weekend at Jim's house. Jim assured her she would have her own bedroom with an en-suite bathroom.

All he had told her was that he had a house with a sea view in Felixstowe. When she first saw it she was completely blown away.

'Oh my god – it's huge. What do you do with all these rooms?'

Jim laughed. 'Oh it's a bit of a punt really. House prices seem like the best long-term investment and I thought that, maybe one day, I'd probably need more space.'

Sally laughed, 'What for – a young wife and several kids?'

Jim looked coy, 'Well, maybe a wife one day but I think I've left it too late for kids. No – I wanted a sea view, it's next to the golf course and I just fell in love with it.'

Sally wandered round the house admiring the sea views and then looked out of a back-bedroom window. 'Wow, you've got a pool - and all that garden. Who looks after all that?'

Jim grinned, 'Not me, I'm too lazy for that. Graham does the pool and the garden and his wife Sue cleans for me a couple of days a week. She does the ironing too – I'm allergic to ironing.'

'Wow, I'm impressed. So what else do you do apart from golf and swimming?'

Jim told her about Seawatch and said that ate up a couple of days a week and had gained him some really good mates who he went to the pub with.

Sally said 'Seawatch sounds interesting – would I be able to visit one day when you're on watch?'

Jim smiled, 'Sure – maybe you'll want to join.'

It wasn't long before Sally stopped using a guest room and moved into the master bedroom with Jim. She loved their long walks, lunches and especially the pool. To say she was impressed was an understatement.

They duly got wed in Guildford and Sally moved to Felixstowe. When Mum and Dad came to stay they were bowled over and thought that after all the disappointments and frustrations their little girl had finally done alright for herself.

Chapter 5

Colin parked his car in the usual spot at the marina, grabbed his back pack and headed for the good ship Tulip. It was more expensive to berth it alongside the wooden jetty but he decided it was worth it not to have to faff around with paddling a dinghy out to a mooring.

He did his usual checks and when he was happy that everything was as it should be, he fired up the engine and cast off. The weather was fine with glimpses of the sun and enough breeze that he fancied getting the sails up. Saskia hadn't wanted to come today as she was spending the day in Bury St Edmunds with a friend.

They would be browsing the boutiques, lunching and maybe a walk through the Abbey Gardens. The nearest big town was Ipswich but the dismal shops, preponderance of eastern Europeans and general tackiness of the town centre held little appeal.

Colin steered Tulip away from the marina and he could already see the giant cranes of Felixstowe further downriver. He liked to check out the vast container ships as he made his way past and on out to sea. Yachts had to keep well clear of the big stuff but he knew the boundaries of the deep-water channel, the recommended tracks for small craft and the crossing points.

It was rare that anyone stepped out of line but when they did the Harbour Authority would be straight on the radio to dish out a severe bollocking. Colin just wanted to keep well clear of trouble, toe the line and enjoy a quiet time to himself.

When passing the Seawatch lookout that reminded him to check-out his radio. He called them up and requested a radio check. They responded that he was loud and clear and he asked whether they were expecting a busy morning. A cheery voice said there would be the usual container ship movements, two dredgers shuttling in and out and various smaller cargo ships. Colin thanked him and promised to keep well clear of the deep-water channel.

He hauled the mainsail up the mast, watched it fill with wind and settled on a course for Cobbolds Point, which marked the turning point to head for the Ferry end of Felixstowe. There were just two other yachts nearby – similar to Tulip. Most of the yachts to be seen in the whole area were white hulled with a single mast and white sails – Bermudan sloops.

Looking to his left Colin could see home. The block of apartments was clearly visible high up on the seafront and theirs was on the top floor. He found it a comfortable home with fantastic views but knew it hadn't been a wise investment.

A neighbour had told him about the article in The Times but when he went to read it at home those two pages had gone missing. He knew Sas must have been distressed to read it and she had decided to try to shield him from such bleak news. He thought it was big of her as she had always wanted a detached house – at least four bed, two bath. He wouldn't have blamed her if she had brandished the story in front of him and said that if it wasn't for his sodding boat they wouldn't be in this mess. But she hadn't and so he wouldn't mention it either.

They would just have to live with it. He had always been one for moving on after any problem. What's done is done – if you can't change it then just accept it and get on with life.

He changed course slightly to starboard to head further out to sea, set the auto pilot and went into the galley to put the kettle on. He knew he could safely make a mug of coffee without coming near anything in sight.

He took the coffee back on deck and settled himself at the helm for a bit of quiet 'me' time. Colin liked being on his own. Sas was different – always wanting friends around her, always on the phone. He accepted she was an extrovert and he was an introvert but he liked it that way. He always thought it a positive thing that he liked his own company – he figured he was pretty content with who he was and felt sorry for people who he thought didn't much like themselves.

He wished Sas would like the sea more though. It was okay when they used the boat's engine to potter up and down the river but he liked what he called the cloth engine – getting the sails up and using a yacht as it was intended to be used.

At first he had been annoyed with Sas and thought she hadn't tried hard enough to get used to a bit of movement on the sea but there was no pleasure in it for either of them if she was just going to be hanging over the side retching. Still, at least she liked the river cruising and he had become reconciled to that.

He turned to port and headed past the estuary to the River Deben. The entrance to the Deben at Felixstowe Ferry was fraught with danger and he kept well clear of it. Shallow waters, sandbanks and a very fast tidal stream meant that anything losing engine power when passing through there would instantly be in trouble. He turned to starboard and looped around to begin a gentle tack back towards the Orwell.

A Dutch dredger was on its way back into Felixstowe docks having been out to sea to dump its load. It was a constant battle to keep the deep-water channel dredged to a depth that made it safe for the ultra-large container ships. Dredged to a depth of 16.5 metres there still wasn't much clearance between the keel of a 210,000 ton container ship and the seabed.

The dredger would suck the seabed into its hold at phenomenal speed – so quickly that when watching from the shore you could visibly seeing it getting lower in the water minute by minute. Colin mused that it must be pretty boring spending all day going backwards and forwards between the docks and the spoil ground area. He had heard that in the old days the captains would cut corners by just dumping their load anywhere once out of sight of the shore. Modern technology meant that a GPS system would record exactly when and where the captain pressed the button to let each load go.

When he neared Landguard Point he lowered the sail and would rely on the engine to get him back to the marina. He watched the cranes loading and unloading the containers and marvelled at the level of automation that kept track of which container was where. With his IT background he wondered what would happen if some disaster occurred that crippled the system and all the back-ups were unusable. He figured that somewhere at some time this must have happened and that it would be as big an IT disaster as the shipping world had ever experienced.

He had once talked to one old boy at the yacht club who used to be the captain of one of the first small container ships. He'd said that he had a model of the ship in his cabin and a load of matchboxes representing the containers. He would shuffle the matchboxes around to work out what to put where, dependent on when and where and in what order they would need to be moved.

Colin grinned to himself at the thought of the modern-day captain of an 'ultra-large' shuffling umpteen thousand matchboxes around.

He entered the marina and came alongside the jetty. He had perfected a technique of getting his bow-rope looped around a cleat on the jetty, using the engine to move the stern in and then repeating the exercise with the stern-rope. You didn't want to jump on the jetty, get things wrong and see your boat drifting away on its own – very embarrassing!

Having tidied up and locked the cabin he headed for the marina clubhouse. He headed for the bar and ordered a pint of Ghost Ship, his favourite local brew. He looked at the special's board, ordered steak and ale pudding and took a seat at a table on his own. He had no weight worries- he had always been stick thin no matter what. There were only three other people there, none of whom he had more than a nodding acquaintance with.

He browsed through The Times and then turned to the crossword – a daily pleasure. The girl behind the bar duly delivered his pudding and he tucked in. As Sas was lunching out he would have his main meal now and then they would both only need a snack at the end of the day.

It was a big plate full of food and when he'd finished there was no room for any dessert. He wandered over to the notice board to see if there was anything of interest.

In amongst the various ads for boats and equipment for sale, chandlery services and the usual bits and pieces was a notice headed 'Seawatch Talk'. It stated that next Wednesday a member of Felixstowe Seawatch would be giving a talk on their role and responsibilities. Given that all the yachties thought they did a good job of looking out for them and could be called on the marine radio for radio checks and local weather reports etc. he thought it would probably be interesting and made a note of it.

Sas had been asking questions about just who Seawatch were and what they did and so maybe she would like to come with him. They could get there early, have a bite to eat and a drink and listen to the talk.

Chapter 6

Jim checked that he had his laptop, projector and all the right leads. It was his turn to do the Seawatch talk tonight at the yacht club. He liked doing these – a one hour Power-point presentation which he had given before to other yacht clubs, U3A, the Lions and Rotary clubs, the WI and various other local groups.

Usually he had a half-interested audience and fielded a number of questions after the talk. He took fliers to hand out which explained more about Seawatch and how people could find out more. On average one or two of the attendees would have a real interest in joining and the talks generally served a dual purpose. Whatever group it was always made a financial donation to Seawatch and also it had gained a number of new watchkeepers from doing these talks over the years.

Sally hadn't wanted to come with him as she had heard it all before and was going to the cinema with a friend. She gave him a peck on the cheek as he loaded up the Merc and set off.

Jim was pleased with the turnout – just over twenty people – a mix of men and women, a couple he recognised but most he didn't.

The club captain introduced him and he launched into his spiel. It seemed to go down well and there were half a dozen questions from the audience at the end. The captain gave a vote of thanks and everyone politely applauded.

Jim packed everything away and made sure he'd got all his leads and connectors. He put everything in the boot of the car and headed for the bar. About half of the attendees had stayed on for a drink and as soon as Jim had got his G&T he found himself fielding more questions.

There were a couple perched on bar stools next to him who seemed keen to find out more. A slim dark-haired chap introduced himself as Colin and asked about the number of watchkeepers, the watch hours and what sort of backgrounds the watchkeepers came from.

Jim couldn't help but notice what he assumed was Colin's wife, sat next to him. A really good looking tallish dark-haired woman in a tight blouse and what was probably a knee-length skirt that was hitched up to allow her to be comfortable on the high stool. She had a look of Kristin Scott-Thomas about her. Jim couldn't resist a sneaky glance at the glimpse of thigh and her knee-high black boots. Definitely an interesting lady!

Colin grinned. 'Sorry, I should have introduced my wife Saskia.'

They both smiled and nodded.

Saskia said 'I liked your talk. I always wondered what you guys get up to in that lookout. You're on top of that office block aren't you, near the nature reserve?'

Jim nodded. 'That's right – people often confuse us with Coastwatch. They're a similar organisation with a lookout station on top of the old Martello tower. They're a lot bigger and, to be honest, more experienced than us.'

She nodded. 'Is there a need for both of you? Aren't you in competition with each other?'

'Yeah, we are to some extent but I think both organisations take the view that you can't have too many people looking out for people in trouble. Also we both have slightly different fields of view so they might see something we don't and vice versa.

Fortunately there are a lot of people in the area who want to get involved with something like this and so there's enough volunteers for both of us. A couple of our watchkeepers are ex-Coastwatch people. They were instrumental in setting our lookout up and putting all the training in place. We've learnt a lot from the Coastwatch people.'

Colin said, 'Yeah, as a yachtie I don't think we can have too many people keeping an eye on us. You guys might save my life one day.'

Jim smiled. 'Well you should both come up some time when I'm on watch and then you can see what we do first-hand. If anyone is even half interested in joining we suggest they first make a visit to see what goes on. If they are still interested they can arrange to do a watch, just as an observer – they don't have to do anything other than see what happens on a typical watch and ask whatever questions they might have.

Some people decide it's not for them because they don't want to make the commitment of doing regular watches or maybe they don't want the hassle of all the training.'

Colin nodded. 'So does much happen on a typical watch?'

'To be honest, no – particularly during the winter. Maybe some people think it would get really boring as nothing untoward happens on the vast majority of watches. But we put the kettle on and chat and it's easy to pass the time. If somebody decides they do want to join they just fill in the application form and get themselves a uniform.'

Saskia smiled, 'and what is the uniform?'

Jim was tempted to reply that what she was wearing now would be okay with him but instead he gave the official response.

'A white pilot shirt, dark tie, dark trousers and dark shoes. Actually there is an online shop – the prices are cheap and people also buy sweaters, body warmers, jackets and stuff if they want.'

Colin said 'I've got a yacht that I keep at the marina here. When I go out I always call up you guys for a radio check and bits of local info. It's a useful service you provide. Maybe we could come up for a visit if you let me know when you're on watch.'

'Yeah sure – if you give me your email address I'll give you my watch dates over the next few weeks.'

Colin fished a business card out of his wallet and handed it over. Jim glanced at it – 'Oh you live in that new block – must be fantastic views from up there.'

Colin nodded, 'Yeah, we're on the top floor so we spend a lot of time sitting on the balcony, ship spotting through the bins. Usually with a beer or a large G&T.'

Jim laughed, 'Good practice for joining Seawatch then!'

Saskia chimed in, 'you say it is usually quiet on watch. What sort of incidents have you been involved in?'

Jim leaned back and thought. 'Probably only two life or death ones – both involving kayaks. The first one was a guy I watched one Sunday morning. He unloaded his kayak from the roof of his car not that far from our lookout. It was blowing about force 3 or 4 and he paddled out a few hundred yards and then got tipped out by a wave. We've got some really powerful bins fixed to a stand and I watched him trying to get back in. He couldn't and so he tried to swim one handed towards the shore, pulling his kayak behind him. He made decent progress at first but I could see he was getting knackered and the tide was turning and he was just getting carried further and further out.'

Saskia looked interested, 'so what did you do?'

'I contacted the Coastguard and they tasked the Harwich lifeboat. They don't have a great view at sea level on the lifeboat and so I talked to them over the radio and conned them to where he was. They duly found him, hauled him out of the water and took him and his kayak back to shore.'

Saskia nodded, 'and was he okay?'

'Yeah, bloody cold and totally knackered, but he was okay.'

Saskia took it in, 'and what was the other kayak incident?'

Jim thought back 'that was a bit different. It was another guy who fell out and couldn't get back in but I couldn't see him. He was in the Felixstowe dock area and luckily he had a real marine radio – not just a mobile phone like a lot of them. He issued a mayday call, explained what had happened but he was really panicky – the water was cold and he knew he needed help fast. The problem was there was no response to his mayday – the Coastguard couldn't hear him.'

Colin said, 'That figures – he's at sea level, Dover Coastguard are probably best part of a hundred miles away and you're just a couple of miles away.'

Jim nodded. 'That's right – so I called Dover, passed on the mayday, explained his position and they immediately tasked the lifeboat. He was fished out five minutes later. It was a good one for us because it showed we could help to save someone even though we couldn't see them.'

Saskia said, 'Well that proves it's worthwhile – if you can save just one life every few years then it's worth doing. What other incidents have you been involved in?'

Jim scratched his head. 'Oh, just yachts running aground on the Deben bar, which we've seen on our CCTV system. That happens just about every month. We can summon help and often they get pulled off but sometimes they don't seem that bothered – more embarrassed than anything. They often just wait for the tide to get them back afloat. One guy was well and truly aground so he jumped over the side with a bucket and scrubber and was cleaning his keel.'

Colin laughed, 'Cheaper than getting the boatyard to crane it out.'

Jim finished his pint and climbed down off his stool. 'Well, it was good to meet you both and I'm glad you found it of interest. I'll email those dates to you. Bye.'

They both thanked him and promised to get in touch.

Back at home Sally asked him how it went.

'Oh fine, about twenty there and I think we might get one or two new recruits from it. How was the film?'

Sally replied 'Oh not bad – no Oscar winner but it was a laugh. Did you stay for a drink with anyone after your talk?'

'Yeah, just had a G&T with a couple who seemed fairly interested in what we do – I think they might join.'

Chapter 7

Today was an unusual day. Sally asked if Jim was golfing but he said he'd give it a miss as none of his regular golfing buddies could make it.

'Well, why don't you play on your own and I could caddy for you?'

Jim smiled, 'Nice idea but won't you be bored?'

'No, it will be a walk and I thought you could settle my caddies fee by buying me lunch in the clubhouse after.'

Jim laughed. 'It's a deal.'

The round didn't start well as Jim put too much fade on his tee shot at the first and they watched the ball curl round and drop straight in the middle of a gorse bush.

'Bloody gorse – so that's three off the sodding tee. Great start!'

He picked up a shot at the second and third holes but had a sense of humour failure at the fourth. A good seven iron landed nicely on the green and two Labradors thought it would be fun to play with the ball. They were being walked by a woman on the coast path.

'Hey, your dogs ought to be on a lead' shouted Jim.

Sally just laughed and started patting the dogs, which didn't improve his mood.

'Lighten up Jimbo', she said. 'You're not playing in The Open.'

Things improved from then on – a few more poor tee shots but some good mid irons and wedges and for once Jim's putter was working. He ended up two over his 15 handicap and was pleased with their morning.

They'd chatted all the way round and Jim kept ribbing Sally for her hopeless guesses at yardages.

Jim had a quick shower in the locker-room while Sally titivated herself and they met up at the bar.

They perused the menu over glasses of a very nice white Rioja and both ordered salads. Jim decided he had been so good that he deserved the sticky toffee pudding but Sal patted her paunch and declined.

They walked home and Sal made coffee, which they had sitting by the pool. Jim started to read the paper but promptly fell asleep. Sal read her latest Jack Reacher book, trying not to be put off by Jim's gentle snoring.

Colin and Saskia were back on their balcony – chatting and ship spotting. Two giant blue Maersk container ships crossed – one delivering a shipload of cheap Chinese products for the UK while the other headed back east to collect yet more. The dredger was still shuttling back and forth and a small trawler was being followed by the usual flock of gulls.

Colin put down the bins and said, 'So what did you think of the Seawatch talk the other day?'

Saskia stretched out her long legs and put her feet up on the rail.

'Yeah, it was good – they seem like a worthy bunch of old boys doing a useful job.'

She laughed. 'It keeps them off the streets I guess.'

Colin chuckled, 'Yes, there is that. Do you think it's worth taking up his offer and paying them a visit? Jim has emailed me with his watch dates. He says we could look around, see what goes on and he'd make us a coffee.'

Saskia sipped her coffee. 'Yeah, why not. We could walk there along the front and it would be something to do.'

Colin grinned, 'I'm sure he'd be glad to see you again – especially your legs.'

Sas laughed. 'What do you mean by that?'

'Well, he was definitely clocking them when you were sat at the bar. He's obviously a leg man.'

Sas laughed. 'Not everyone is like you.'

Colin picked up the bins again to look at the Harwich pilot boat heading out. 'I don't know if I'd want to join but you might – it could give you a new interest.'

Saskia thought about what he'd said. 'I don't know if I'd take to it. I've watched you plotting positions and courses and stuff and never had a clue how you do it. I don't know that I've got any aptitude for it.'

Colin responded with 'Sounds like they've got some really good self-study training. You could learn a lot of it sitting at the PC in the study. I could probably help with any stuff you find tricky and you could do some practical work on the boat. It might make going out on Tulip more interesting for you – you'd understand a lot more about boating in general.'

Saskia smiled. 'I don't see how it would help my seasickness problem.'

Colin thought about it. 'Well they do say that one of the best things to help you avoid it is to keep busy. Maybe you are just sitting on your backside in the boat wondering how you are feeling and that isn't helping you.'

Saskia didn't look convinced.

That evening Colin called Jim and they agreed that he and Sas would come up to the lookout when Jim was on watch on Sunday morning.

Sally had also been thinking about something new she could join. She wanted to get more involved with the local community and had been looking at notices in the library.

Someone had suggested the local Horticultural Society but as she hated gardening that didn't make any sense. She browsed fliers about U3A, the rotary club, pilates classes, yoga, the book club, the folk music scene and then stumbled upon the local Amateur Dramatic Society.

She had tried some keep fit classes and pilates but everyone seemed so old and the exercises were so gentle that she figured she got more benefit from just strolling along the front. The one time she had tried yoga she fell asleep and then ended up with backache.

She wondered why the Am Dram idea hadn't come to her before. With her theatrical background it was the obvious thing. Although she'd always regarded herself as a professional actress she thought it might be fun to get involved in something she might actually shine at. She wouldn't have to tell anyone about her past life and hopefully they would be impressed when they saw what she could do. There would be no pressure and it might just be her chance to take a leading role after all the years of bit parts.

Over dinner that night she discussed it with Jim.

'Great idea Sal. I think it would be good for you. Don't expect me to join but I'd love to see you back on the stage again. You'd be a knockout.'

Sally grinned. 'I doubt that but at least I don't think I'd embarrass myself and I'd make some new friends. It will make a change from all those roles as a maid or a policewoman and I wouldn't have to stay in a rat-infested B&B.'

Jim laughed. 'No, I think you've moved on from that sort of life. Get in touch – give it a try.'

Sally poured herself another glass of Sauvignon, sat back on the recliner and reminisced about the old days on the boards. She smiled as she remembered the half empty, pokey little provincial theatres, the new friends who came into her life and then disappeared again at the end of a run.

Most of all she remembered the truly awful accommodation and meals. Always strapped for cash the cast would check out all sorts of options but always the deciding factor was price. She had done a few plays near to home and being able to work while still enjoying home comforts had been bliss. Once, over a plate of egg and chips in a Scarborough boarding house, her companion had trapped a mouse under his shoe. Those were the days she mused.

Chapter 8

Jim climbed the seven flights of steps to the lookout. The standing joke within Seawatch was that if you could actually get up to the lookout then you had passed the medical. It was perched at the top of an old office block used by one of the shipping companies. When they had been approached about the possibility of the top floor being used by Seawatch they eventually decided it was a worthy cause which they should support.

The top floor had been an addition some twenty years previously for storage but it had no proper heating and the staff had been averse to spending any more time up there than they had to. It did have large panoramic windows though and a handful of local boating types had often talked of it being an ideal location for a lookout station.

It had taken a lot of work but a group of willing volunteers with time on their hands had spent many months transforming it. Amongst the first people to get involved were a retired plumber, a carpenter, two electricians, several people who had worked in IT and various others with all sorts of different skills that were useful. They had installed furniture, heaters, computers, a CCTV system, high powered binoculars and mounted a radar aerial on the roof.

Grants from the council, the port authority, various shipping companies, the rotary club, the Lions and many others had helped with all the funding. The venture received a lot of good PR in the local media and it all reflected well upon the owners of the building. They charged Seawatch just a peppercorn rent and helped with the installation costs of a small kitchen and a toilet.

Jim had first heard about it when the Station Manager Steve Blake was interviewed on BBC Radio Suffolk. He had talked about what had been achieved, what they did and that they were on the lookout for new volunteers.

He'd been thinking he needed something other than golf to keep him interested. Just about all the household chores were delegated to Sue and Graham and he could only spend so much time eating and drinking. He figured Seawatch would be something completely different that could get him a whole set of new mates.

Jim called the BBC, made contact with Steve and within a month he had visited the tower, done a watch, acquired his uniform and become a fully-fledged Trainee Watchkeeper.

 He quickly settled in and made a start on completing the training papers which would familiarise him with everything in the very comprehensive training manual. A lot of it he already knew from his boating experience and from the RYA courses he had attended. Some of it was completely new to him though and it felt good to be learning again.

He usually stood one watch a week – with a variety of different people, both male and female. There was an online booking system for the watches and he usually left it late and booked himself on with somebody he knew was good company.

Jim preferred the morning watches at weekends – 0900 to 1300. He was a morning person - always awake early, he enjoyed busy mornings and relaxing afternoons.

Today he was on with Mike Ford – a fellow yachtsman who kept his boat at the same marina as Colin used for Tulip. Mike had been in Seawatch for a couple of years and had quickly worked through the papers to progress to Senior Watchkeeper. He'd had a lifetime's association with the sea – working in the docks and spending many years as the skipper of a tug.

Mike bemoaned the continuous drive for efficiencies, which really meant cost cutting. When he had first become a deckhand on a tug there had been a crew of six but this was gradually whittled down to three – the skipper, a deckhand and an engineer. By the time he retired the company was dispensing with the engineers – arguing that modern tugs were much like cars when it came to operating and utilising the engines.

Wages were being driven down and Mike was relieved just to get out and start drawing his pension. He'd always been a saver, his wife Maureen had always worked and they both entered into the retired boat-owner world with enthusiasm.

They switched all the equipment on, reported in to the Coastguard and did a radio check. Mike started the official log in which they would record the details of the weather, tide times and all of the vessels and any incidents they might see.

Jim raised the Seawatch flag on the little mast on the roof and they were ready for business. They both took their first detailed scan of the coastline and the seascape through binoculars. Mike was using the big fixed bins and Jim the ordinary self-focussing ones. He always marvelled at how they worked – no matter what state your eyes were in the bins somehow adjusted so that you got a good field of vision. No twiddling with rotary eyepieces or levers - they just worked. He often wondered why opticians couldn't use similar technology for glasses. Maybe it was all part of a huge conspiracy! The bins weren't even very expensive.

They heard the captain of the Stena Hollandica requesting permission to leave Harwich. It left every morning on its daily trip to the Hook of Holland. The captain enquired about traffic in the area and reported that there were 514 people on board.

He would have loved to be on board, setting off on one of their European driving holidays. The weather was warm, the sea flat and he mused that they could be having a cosy dinner by the canal in Utrecht by evening.

Jim looked around to see which cranes were operating and then got on the computer to see what movements were planned for Felixstowe port that day.

He looked at Mike. 'That big Maersk on 8&9 is getting ready to leave and then an Evergreen is due in to take her place. There are a couple of tiddlers due in and the usual roll on – roll off ferry.'

Jim put the kettle on and made them both coffee. They listened to the routine radio traffic, checked the CCTV images of the Deben and waved to the volunteer lifeboat as it passed close inshore on its first patrol of the day. A couple of yachts called in for radio checks and the first kayaker ventured out.

As he scanned the seafront he could see Colin and Saskia strolling toward the tower. He studied them through the big bins and was a little disappointed to see Saskia in jeans and a casual shirt – there would be no opportunity to see those legs today. Jim went into the little toilet, combed his hair in the mirror and checked his shirt was properly tucked in.

'We're going to get some visitors soon Mike. A couple who came to the last talk I did at the yacht club. They seemed interested and want to have a look around - see what we do.'

Mike looked through the bins. 'Yeah I see them – she's a tidy looking girl.'

Jim smiled to himself and thought that yep, that was one way of describing Saskia. He headed down the stairs to meet them.

They all made the usual pleasantries about the climb up to the lookout and Jim tried not to puff and pant too much. He made the introductions and Mike said he'd make coffees for Colin and Saskia while Jim told them what was what.

They gazed out of the window. 'Wow', said Colin, 'what a view – it's like our view from the apartment but I guess it's more interesting being able to see the dock area. You get a closer view of the big ships turning into the estuary.'

Jim agreed. 'Yes, you must get a great view. My place is just two storeys and although we've got a sea view we can't see down to the shoreline.'

Both Colin and Saskia seemed genuinely interested and asked loads of questions. They were impressed by the bins and the CCTV pictures of the Deben area.

66

Colin asked, 'If you see anyone in trouble down there can you zoom in on them and get a bearing?'

'Yes', said Jim, 'The camera's got a forty-times zoom and we can move it around wherever we want. These modern systems are very clever. Its got a wiper so we can keep it clean and it's almost vandal proof. It would be really difficult for any yob armed with a few bricks to put it out of action. If it wasn't for the data protection act I'd be able to look at my house.'

Saskia laughed, 'what do you mean, why can't you?'

Jim explained that they had to program the camera software so that it blanked out all the houses in the area.

Saskia laughed, 'so no chance of spotting your wife doing anything she shouldn't.'

Jim laughed and privately thought that he wouldn't mind being able to see into Saskia's bedroom.

After about an hour of chat Colin said they'd have to be making a move as they were taking Tulip out for a little lunchtime cruise along the Orwell.

'So what do you both think?' said Jim. 'Do you think you'd be interested in joining?'

Colin smiled and looked quizzically at Saskia. 'I don't think I've got the time but I think Sas might be interested.'

Sas looked unsure. 'I might be but I don't know about all this plotting stuff - courses and bearings and stuff I don't know anything about. I don't think I'd be very good at judging distances and I've never had to learn about radio procedure and stuff like that.'

'Lots of our people were like that to start with', said Jim. 'But it comes with experience – you get used to the local landmarks and after a while you know how far away the various buoys, headlands and the pier are and you can gauge distances from that. The training is really good and there are no time pressures. Some people work through all the training papers in six months and some still haven't done them all after six years – it's up to you.'

Saskia looked unconvinced. 'I don't know – you probably don't realise just how clueless I am when it comes to the sea. I'd hate to make some terrible mistake when there is an emergency out there – I could cost somebody their life.'

Jim smiled. 'Why not just think about it. You could do a lot of the training by self-study. Sitting at home with your tablet and quizzing Colin if you don't get something.'

She thought about it. 'You said before that people can do a watch as an observer before making their mind up and taking the plunge. I think I might do that but I don't want to make any promises about joining yet.'

'That's not a problem – you could do that and then if you think it's not for you then that's perfectly okay. If you decide you do want to join then you fill in the application form and we take it from there. There is absolutely no pressure – we don't want anyone to join unless they are convinced they really want to give it a go.'

'Okay', said Sas. 'I'll think about it'.

They both thanked Jim and Mike for their time and the coffee and said their goodbyes.

Jim studied them through the bins as they made their way back along the prom and mused that she really did have a cute bum. He realised he'd be very disappointed if she decided against joining.

'Nice couple', said Mike. 'I think you might have got a new recruit there.'

'We can but hope', said Jim.

Chapter 9

The one little niggle in Jim's past that he lived with, day in – day out, dated back nearly twenty years now. No matter how often he told himself it was nothing – anyone would have grabbed the opportunity he was presented with – he couldn't shake the feeling off.

Roy Manning was an old friend from uni days. They had graduated together and Roy had gone straight into IT – or the computer industry as it was known then. Starting as a programmer with one of the big manufacturers he had progressed into management. He ran a team that developed accounting systems for big blue-chip companies.

They met up at annual reunions but didn't see much of each other between times. After a few years Roy decided to branch out and start his own software business. Working with two friends they formed Data Finance, based in a pokey office in the east end of London.

Five years later there were nearly a hundred employees working out of a modern office block in Reading. The software they developed was now widely used across the financial world. They had grown partly through their own efforts and partly through the acquisition of other businesses they had some synergy with.

Jim had a number of growing IT businesses in his client list, for whom his business were providing accounting services and also some management consultancy.

Roy was an urbane type – a smart casual dresser with longish brown hair framing a confident looking face. He'd put on a bit of weight over the years but otherwise had aged well. It was at one of the reunions that they compared notes on how things were at work.

'So, how are things with you Jim? Still making a fortune from the accountancy world?'

Jim laughed. 'Not a fortune exactly but enough to keep the wolf from the door.'

Roy smiled, 'You always were one for understatement so I'll take that as a yes. Still building your client list?'

'Yeah – things change pretty fast, as you well know. There's a lot of new products around – people doing some clever stuff. I used to think that if you had a good product range and a solid client list you knew you were safe for at least a couple of years but not now. You can be totally happy with your lot and then six months down the line you're wondering how the hell it all went tits-up.'

Roy nodded. 'Yep, tell me about it, it's change, change, change but if it wasn't then my business would stagnate. We just have to try and thrive off change and hope we're getting most things right. What I've found is that for us, very often, when we have half an idea for a development project it's best to look around for somebody who's already doing it. Taking over a business might be expensive but it can save you a fortune in the long run, if it's the right business. If we look to copy somebody's idea we are always going to be behind them and then when we finally get the product to market we've left it too late.'

Jim agreed. 'We've got a couple of clients who are in the same sector as you and I'm working with one of them now. They are developing some new data acquisition software – it's really clever stuff. Or, at least, it looks clever to me.'

Roy's ears pricked up. 'What does it do?'

'Well, basically it's a way of searching through the whole of a company's email traffic, finding stuff relating to a common theme. You get different individuals in different business units touching on something that the business decides to get into but there's no coordination. Nobody knows what else has been done in the rest of the organisation on that particular topic.'

Roy was really interested now. 'You mean company X might decide to develop something relating to say, electric car battery charging systems, and they want to know what sort of knowledge base they have about that market across the whole company?'

Jim nodded. 'That's right. One department might have looked at the technology, another at the financials, another has looked at what competitors are doing. A lot of it is totally random – one email might have a technical research paper attached to it and another might just be someone emailing a colleague to say his electric car had broken down and he thought the battery charger was crap. They've probably got quite a bit of information but there's been no easy way to link it all up. This software searches through all of the emails, groups them and analyses them. It's a sort of search engine looking through everybody's emails for related keywords, in clever ways.'

Roy nodded. 'Yeah, that's cool. I can really see the need for that. How long have they been working on it?'

'Oh, a couple of years I guess but they are near to bringing it to market now. They plan to launch it in a blaze of publicity and I think the founders are going to make an absolute killing.'

Roy smiled. 'I don't suppose there's any point me asking who they are?'

Jim laughed. 'No, that wouldn't exactly be ethical, would it?'

'Well, can I just ask if they are a listed company or is the ownership with the founders.'

Jim thought before replying, 'Okay, I'll tell you they are listed but I won't say any more.'

They chatted some more about family stuff, golf and the usual small talk before saying their goodbyes.

Jim thought no more about the conversation in the following days but Roy thought a lot about it and at the weekly board meeting he brought it up under AoB. There was general agreement that it sounding really interesting and was something they should try to find out more about.

Roy gave it a few days before phoning Jim. 'Hi Jimbo, Roy here. It was great to see you last week – it made me think we ought to see each other more often instead of just at the reunion once a year.'

'Hi Roy – yeah that would be good but I guess we're both really busy and we aren't exactly neighbours.'

'No, but I'm visiting a client in your neck of the woods next week and wondered if you fancied a round of golf and a lunch, on me.'

Jim knew where this was leading but, off the top of his head, couldn't think of a reason to decline the offer and so arrangements were made for the following Wednesday. He booked the tee time at the Cambridge golf club.

The day dawned overcast but dry with not much wind – good golfing weather. They swapped scorecards on the first tee, noted handicap details, tossed up and Roy hit a pretty good drive down the middle of the first.

After the usual pleasantries about families and holidays Roy was keen to broach the subject of Jim's client with the clever idea.

'I've been thinking about what you said about this client of yours Jim. We've been doing a series of businesses cases on software developers who might be ripe for investing in, or even taking over. We've built up pretty good cash reserves and we would prefer to reinvest it rather than paying out big dividends. I wonder if there's any chance of finding out more about your client?'

Jim hit an okay pitching wedge on to the edge of the sixth green and grinned. 'You know I've got to be so careful what I say Roy. It's a client who we've built up a lot of trust with and there's no way I'm going to risk any allegation of insider dealing.'

Roy missed a long putt by a good six feet and put down his marker. 'It could be that you are doing the client a favour – you might be able to help them and help yourself.'

Jim was wary. 'Well, I know they have a bit of a short-term cash flow problem with bringing the product to market but once they do they are going to be quids in.'

Roy marked his scorecard and cleaned his ball. 'If we made an investment we might solve their cash flow problem, improve our finances and give you some sort of thank you in the form of a consultancy fee.'

Jim sliced his drive down the ninth, swore and leaned on his trolley. 'Bloody hell Roy – that's dodgy ground. I'd never risk my business by doing something that's clearly unethical to say the least. It's probably not just unethical – it might be illegal.'

Roy smiled. 'No, I wouldn't expect you to but it's not as if we'd be ripping anyone off – everyone could come out a winner. As a chartered accountant I'm sure you'd know the most efficient way to do something like this.'

Jim's long iron was as bad as his tee shot – ending up in deep rough. 'I'm a stickler for audit trails Roy – I've never cooked the books and I'd certainly never screw a valued client.'

Roy brushed the clubface grooves on his seven iron. 'Why not just think about it for a few days Jim. I don't want you to do anything you don't want to do but if we could somehow make this work I would be very grateful. I'm sure we could find a way to pay a very generous consultancy fee for your advice.'

By the time they reached the eighteenth Jim was one shot behind but he was savvy enough to figure that Roy would find a way to lose. Sure enough Roy three putted from just fifteen feet and Jim won by one shot.

They dumped their clubs in the cars, showered and headed for the clubhouse. After a pint at the bar they sat down in the restaurant and chose from the menu. Roy chose the steak and kidney pie from the 'specials' and Jim opted for the roast lamb.

Between mouthfuls Roy elaborated on his thoughts. 'I thought that if I shared with you the work we've done on the other developers then there wouldn't be any need to even mention your client. You could be giving us general consultancy advice on our overall investment plans. We could pay you via a sort of 'with profits' fee, relating to the profits we might make from this.'

Jim thought about it. 'I don't know. Maybe that sounds a bit more feasible. It wouldn't be like insider trading I suppose, with dealing directly related to my client's shares. The audit trail is too straightforward if we go down that route – too damn obvious.'

So after a lot more discussion, three meetings, many phone calls, agonising and much questioning, the deed was done. Data Finance did the deal – they paid over the odds for a sizable chunk of Jim's client Davis & Kershaw. Davis & Kershaw were happy in that it gave them the capital to launch the product. The product was indeed an instant success and within a year Davis & Kershaw had been taken over by one of the blue-chip giants of the IT industry. Data Finance made a killing on their shares and

Jim's with-profits consultancy fee amounted to just over a million pounds.

Some of Jim's fee went through the books in the normal way with absolutely no mention of Davis & Kershaw in any paperwork. Other money was carefully sifted through offshore accounts. Back in those days a lot of the money laundering restrictions that came in after the 2008 crash were still to be born. It was much easier to be a little creative without taking unnecessary risks. Further share trades resulted in more windfalls for Jim but he was always ultra-careful. A labyrinth of transactions, transfers and audit trails were used which would have taken a small army of investigators to dissect.

So Jim convinced himself that nobody had lost out. They were all winners in the end. But there was just that tiny little niggle that never went away.

He never shared the story with Sally and she never asked just how her husband had made so much money from a life as an accountant. She just thought that it was normal because, after all, it was a world away from being a jobbing actress.

Chapter 10

Jim was sat in his study when the call came.

'Hi Jim, it's Saskia here. How are you?'

'Great, nice to hear from you. How are you both?'

'We're good thanks – Colin is having a maintenance day on Tulip. Something to do with rigging.'

'Yeah, it's never ending with boats. So what did you think after your visit?'

'I'm interested but not sure yet. Can I take up your offer of doing a watch as an observer?'

'Yes, of course – there's no pressure. Do a watch and then decide. If you don't want to take it any further that's no problem. It will have been nice to have met you anyway.'

'Okay, when are you on next?'

'I'm on again next Saturday morning. Is that any good with you?'

'Yes, it's fine. I know Colin will be out on Tulip - he wants to get the sails up, so it won't be just a river trip. I'll be at a loose end.'

'Okay, great. We could keep an eye out for him and call him up on the radio. Give him a surprise.'

'It's a date Jim, shall I get there just before you open up at 9?'

'Best if you come about a quarter to nine and then you can see what we have to do to get ready first thing. There's a bit of set-up work to do before opening up. We have to switch everything on, check out a few websites, check the radios and generally get ready for the day.'

'Okay Jim. Look forward to it. See you Saturday.'

He leaned back and looked out of the window with a smile on his face. So he would have the lovely Saskia's company for a whole morning.

Sally shouted up, 'want a coffee?'

'Yes please Sal – I'll come down and we can have it by the pool.'

They stretched out on recliners to enjoy the warmth of the sun. It hadn't rained for ages and the grass was turning brown. There were obvious advantages to living in one of the driest areas of the country but sometimes it was worrying. He often wondered how the water board could keep the taps running without introducing any restrictions.

Jim looked at Sally. 'So what do you fancy doing today? I'm not golfing so we could go somewhere for a pub lunch if you like.'

She liked the sound of that. 'How about the Fox? The food's always good there and we could walk around the springs afterwards.'

'Yeah, it's warm enough that we could sit outside. Better take our hats. The last time we went there I had a terrific leek, stilton and potato pie off the specials board. I'm going to have that again if they're still doing it.'

Sally thought about it. She really fancied a salad.

They ate out three or four times a week. Sometimes Sally felt guilty about not cooking more home meals but Jim was more than happy to let someone else do all the work. He liked to say he was doing his bit for the local economy by helping to keep all the chefs and waiters employed.

Sally pushed her sunglasses on to the top of her head. 'I was talking to Carole Bennet who runs the flower club. She's putting on a quiz at the library – wondered if you wanted to enter a Seawatch team.'

'Maybe – how many people?'

'Up to six she said. Nibbles and a glass of wine - £10 a head.'

'When is it?'

'The first Wednesday every month, seven o'clock for seven thirty. I think she's hoping you might make it a regular fixture.'

Jim thought about it. 'I'll talk to a few of the guys and see who's interested. How about you putting together a girly team?'

Sally turned her nose up. 'Nah – don't think so, not keen on quizzes. You boys always take it too seriously.'

Jim laughed. 'That's because we want to win.'

She stood, hitched up her jeans and smoothed her top down. 'Does my bulge show under this?'

'Yes, it's absolutely huge. Unlikely you'll even get through the door at The Fox. I think we might have to give lunch a miss.'

She thumped him in the arm and coffee splashed on the patio. 'Get off your arse and get yourself ready Boris.'

Lunch was as good as usual. Salmon salad for Sally, the leek, stilton and potato pie for Jim and big glasses of Pinot Grigio for both of them. They soaked up the sun and Jim started to drift off to sleep. Sally kicked his leg and said 'walkies'.

The walk around the freshwater springs was always good – well shaded woodland, lots of wild flowers and mostly on a boardwalk. It was a walk for all weathers.

They headed back to the car and Sally said she didn't want to go straight home. She wanted to go into Ipswich to look for a top in M&S.

'Do we have to?' groaned Jim. 'Parking is always a pain and you're always moaning about M&S. I thought you said they didn't cater for anyone other than old dears with no sense of style.'

Sally laughed. 'It's true but Sue said they'd got a new range in and amazingly some of it wasn't half bad. They keep trying to turn things around – one of these days they'll get it right.'

'Or go bust', he retorted.

Neither of them liked Ipswich town centre but sometimes they just had to go there. Felixstowe had few shops and even their little M&S had closed. Ipswich was much bigger but Jim was always scathing about the people.

'Why is this place always full of unemployed eastern Europeans and fat girls waddling around staring at their phones? Why aren't they at work, or at least at the bloody job centre?'

Sally duly checked out M&S and actually bought two tops.

'Bet you'll be taking those back next week', said Jim.

Sally chuckled. 'As if. Tell you what – buy me a coffee and then we can head home.'

They went into Costa – Sally wanted a skinny latte while Jim ordered an Americano with milk.

They sat in grubby looking armchairs that had clearly seen better days. Jim looked around.

'Just about everyone in here looks out of work and obese. Look at those girls – bound to be on benefits, drinking coffee at the best part of three quid and stuffing themselves with chocolate muffins. What's going on?'

'Bloody hell Jimbo – you're in a sunny mood this afternoon. What's up?'

He sighed. 'I just think there's something very wrong when people on benefits can afford to keep on stuffing their bellies while playing with phones on really expensive monthly contracts. People in this country don't know what true poverty is. I bet they go home, order a Chinese takeaway and watch Sky all night.'

Sally stood up, stretched and gave him another kick.

'Come on laughing boy – home time.'

Chapter 11

Jim was on watch with Steve Tomlinson when Saskia came up to do her observation watch. She was looking good in a light blue shirt and dark blue jeans.

Jim introduced her to a clearly impressed Steve.

'Steve - this is Saskia – a possible new recruit. She came to the talk I gave at the yacht club last month and it seems I didn't put her off. She's with us this morning to do an observation watch before she makes her mind up.'

Steve shook hands and grinned. 'We need all the help we can get and a young lady makes a change from all the retired old boys we've got.'

Saskia laughed, 'I'm not so young any more, I'm retired myself.'

Steve looked at her, 'Well compared to us you're a mere slip of a girl.'

Jim said 'Steve used to work in Felixstowe docks, shuffling containers around. He knows a lot more than I do about the shipping world. He's a good guy to learn from.'

Steve chuckled. 'Well Jim here knows plenty enough to be a good watchkeeper. I'll let him tell you what's what and I'll put the kettle on. Coffee or tea?'

'Coffee please, white, no sugar.'

Jim called the Coastguard on the phone and reported that Felixstowe Seawatch was now open for duty. He requested a radio check and this was 'loud and clear', as always.

He showed Saskia the different marine radios and explained how they were tuned in to different channels which were used for different purposes. He switched on the CCTV system, the radar and the large desktop computer.

Steve handed over the coffees and offered Saskia the tin of biscuits.

'No thanks Steve. I'll pass.'

He looked down at his big beer belly. 'You'll never get to be like me if you don't eat biscuits and have sugar in your coffee.'

Jim laughed, 'I don't think she wants to be like you Steve.'

He looked at Saskia. 'Steve's wife Trudy is a really prodigious cook – that's how he came to look like that. She dishes out enormous helpings of lovely home cooked food and he can't ever say no.'

Jim showed Saskia what sort of things they had to log. He got her to guess what the sea state and swell was and the amount of cloud cover. They logged the times of the tides, the barometer readings and the temperature.

A yacht came out of the Orwell and Steve explained how to log its details.' She is a bermuda rigged sloop, white hull, white sails, the sail number is GB3872, we can see three people on board, she's heading north east and I'll show you how we log her position.'

Saskia said 'It looks similar to Colin's boat but he doesn't have a number on the sail. But Tulip is single masted and all white.'

'That's what most of the yachts are like here – probably ninety percent are what we call YBSs – that is the rig code for a 'yacht Bermudan sloop.'

'Why do you bother to log the vessels?' asked Saskia.

'Well, it could be useful if a boat goes missing. If we had it logged at a certain time in a certain place then that could be useful information in a search and rescue exercise.'

They used the computer to look at the schedule of ships going in and out and Jim pointed out a particularly big new Maersk container ship that was due in that evening. 'If you and Colin are sat on your balcony with a drink tonight you want to keep an eye out for that one. It's 225,000 tons – just about the biggest container ship in the world right now. It's come from China but she stopped off in Hamburg on the way here.'

Saskia looked through the big binoculars on the stand. 'No sign of Tulip out there – maybe Colin had a problem with whatever he's been doing on the rigging. There's a big black container ship out there – looks like it's coming in.'

Jim looked and read the bearing of it before looking at the computer. He quickly found it on the screen, clicked the mouse on the little boat symbol and up came all the information.

'It's the MSC Coburg – 68,000 tons. It's just come from Singapore. Have a look.'

Saskia saw a range of pictures on the screen showing the Coburg from all angles and was suitably impressed.

'You got all this up from a click of the mouse?'

'Yeah, it's amazing what you can do these days. I can find out what the Captain had for breakfast.'

She laughed and punched him playfully on the arm.

He showed her how to get all the current weather data, the met office inshore waters forecast and the wealth of stuff on the Seawatch website. 'This is where all the self-study training material is but you don't want to look at that yet. If you want to join you can just do that in your own time – as fast or as slow as you want.'

She looked at the chart. 'I'm really not sure about all this plotting malarkey Jim.'

'Don't worry – we can do that together if you do come on board. We could get you really proficient over several watches and then you could amaze Colin when you are out on Tulip. You could take a couple of compass bearings, use a thing called a Yeoman plotter, which Colin is sure to have, and show him the exact position of the boat on his chart.'

She squeezed his arm and gave him a big smile. 'Oh that would be great – he'd be absolutely gobsmacked. I could look all cool – like I'd been doing it all my life. Do you reckon I could do that?'

'I'm absolutely certain you can.'

She squeezed harder and looked into his eyes like an excited little girl. Jim smiled and blushed, like a very excited and somewhat stunned old-age pensioner.

She left her hand there just a little bit longer than was really necessary and Jim knew Seawatch had got a new recruit.

Chapter 12

Colin brought coffee out on to the balcony where Saskia was sitting back on a chair with her feet up on the rail. The weather wasn't perfect but it was still warm with occasional glimpses of the sun.

She sipped her coffee and looked at her husband. 'So what happened to you today – didn't you get out at all?'

'No, I had a problem with the new rigging – it was a real pain in the arse. I needed a shackle which the chandlery didn't have in stock until the end of the afternoon. But I've got it now – fitted it and she's ready for sea again.'

'I kept an eye out for you – I was going to surprise you by calling you on the radio – if Jim had let me. So what did you do all day?'

'Fiddled about, did some jobs, washed the deck and had a pint in the clubhouse. Dozed off over the crossword and had a bite to eat. How about you – how was Seawatch?'

'It was good, really enjoyed it. Jim showed me what was what and the other chap on watch was a really nice old boy. I'm going to fill in the application form and if they'll have me then I'll get my uniform.'

Colin grinned. 'Good stuff – it will really get you into the nautical world – you'll soon be champing at the bit to get out to sea with me. I'll be able to have a G&T and a snooze in the cabin while you take charge. You can navigate and take the helm.'

She laughed. 'Don't get carried away. I do think I'll understand a bit more about what's going on though.'

She picked up the binoculars to examine a big blue ship on the horizon. 'That's a big Maersk on the way in – I reckon it's about 225,000 tons.'

Colin spluttered his mouthful of coffee down the arm of his shirt. 'What? You haven't got a clue what tonnage it is. You haven't instantly become a ship recognition expert after your first watch.'

She grinned. 'I bet I'm right – I can see the size of it from here.'

Colin laughed. 'Bollocks – you're just making that up.'

'So do you want to have a bet on it?'

He couldn't believe what he was hearing. 'Sure, I'll bet you a tenner you aren't within 10,000 tons.'

She laughed. 'Okay, it's a bet. Check it out.'

Colin grabbed his phone and looked at the ship tracking website.

'Well, you're right about one thing – it is a Maersk. It's the Adriana Maersk.'

'I know it is – now check out her details.'

He studied his phone and then spluttered 'Bloody hell, it's 224,768 tons. How the hell did you do that?'

She laughed. 'Oh, it just looks about 225,000 to me. I think you'll find that's a tenner you owe me.'

Colin grunted. 'Okay, you've set me up. Very clever – I suppose you've learnt how to look at the Felixstowe port sailing schedule website?'

'Yeah, you'll be surprised what I might learn at Seawatch. Maybe I'll teach you a thing or two.'

He grinned. 'That's great – I'll be really chuffed if you do. I think it's going to be really good for you. So how did you get on with Jim? I bet he's happy to have some female company up there.'

'Oh fine – yeah he's a nice guy. When I get to know him a bit better I'd like to meet his wife.'

Colin nodded. 'Yeah, the four of us could have a meal together. We could invite them here – show off our sea view.'

'I don't know if they'd be that impressed – they live in one of those big houses near the golf club. But he's got no airs or graces – just seems like a regular guy.'

'How did he make enough money to buy one of those places?'

Saskia thought about it. 'Don't really know. He's an accountant – I think he had a firm in the City. He lived in Stanmore – that's a really well-heeled area. He certainly wouldn't have found Felixstowe expensive. He wanted out though and moved here a few years back. He hasn't been married all that long – his wife is an arty type.'

Colin was half listening – half browsing stuff on his phone. 'She fell on her feet meeting him then.'

Saskia looked thoughtful. 'You don't know that – maybe she's the one with the money. Maybe he got lucky meeting her.'

Colin chuckled. 'Unlikely – if she'd made a fortune from whatever arty stuff she was doing we'd probably have heard of her. I don't think many arty types are rolling in it.'

Saskia studied an old sailing barge through the bins. 'Well, lets invite them to dinner and see what we can find out. Jim's easy enough and his wife sounds nice from what he says.'

Colin nodded. 'No probs - organise something when you're on with him next.'

Chapter 13

Over the next few weeks Saskia did a number of watches –
mostly with Jim but one with Mike and one with Steve.

Jim just knew she would look really good in her new uniform
and she did. A crisp white shirt and narrow legged black trousers
– not like the enormous wide trousers most of the men wore. She
had bought the official Seawatch tie and with her new name
badge on she looked the business.

She quickly got to grips with all the basics of watchkeeping and
had made a start on the online training. She successfully
completed the first two training papers and Colin was pleased
when she asked him for help with various things.

When they went out on Tulip he could see she had more interest.
She would study the chart and identify buoys and landmarks –
things she had never previously shown any interest in.

One day when they anchored in the Orwell for lunch he was
absolutely amazed when she plotted their position on the chart.
He watched as she took compass bearings on a buoy, a church
steeple and a tower and plotted them on the chart in the cabin.

The three lines neatly intersected and she proudly stated 'that's
where we are.'

Colin checked and she was spot on. 'Wow Sas – that's fantastic,
well done you.'

She grinned – pleased with herself. 'There's no telling what I'll be able to do after a few months at Seawatch.'

Colin laughed. 'You'll be plotting courses as we head out to sea. We could go over to Holland or France.'

Saskia shook her head. 'Don't get carried away. It still won't solve my seasickness problem.'

One afternoon she was telling Jim about how she had been able to impress Colin.

'He's so pleased and I must admit this has made going out on Tulip a lot more interesting for me. We wondered if you and Sally would like to join us for dinner at ours one evening.'

Jim was only too ready to accept. 'Yeah, that would be great. Give me a date that suits both of you and I'll run it past Sal.'

She rang him the following day and they agreed on the Friday evening at seven'o'clock.

Sally asked her usual question. 'What shall I wear?'

Jim grinned. 'Whatever – they're a nice couple, very laid back. I'm sure they won't dress up.'

Sally wasn't sure. 'Tell me more about them – what do they look like?'

Jim thought. 'Colin is tallish, quite slim, a good head of dark hair, quite good looking I guess. Saskia is also on the tall side, slim, darkish hair – I guess they really look like a couple.'

'Is she pretty?'

'Yeah I guess so – she's neat and tidy.'

Sally laughed. 'Neat and tidy – what a typically blokeish thing to say when you think someone's gorgeous. Is she sexy?'

Jim looked ever so slightly flustered. 'I suppose she would be to some people – she's quite good looking I guess.'

'Quite good looking eh? Do you fancy her?'

Jim laughed. 'I've got enough on my plate with you.'

She smiled. 'I think I'll wear those new white trousers with the blue top and a light jacket. We better take flowers and wine. What are you going to wear?'

'Absolutely no idea. I'll look in the wardrobe on Friday.'

The weather was improving as they left spring behind and it really started to feel like summer. Friday turned out nice and they agreed to walk so they could both drink.

Sally had bought roses, alstroemeria and some greenery - she wrapped rustic looking brown paper around them and tied it all up with raffia. Jim picked out a particularly good bottle of Cote du Rhone.

They got the lift up to the top floor and rang the doorbell. Saskia opened the door looking absolutely stunning. She'd obviously had her hair done and was wearing a short flowery dress and sandals. She loved the flowers and thanked them for the wine.

Colin appeared looking cool in shirt and chinos and all the introductions were made. He led the way into the lounge and both Jim and Sally were impressed by the classy modern furniture and tasteful pictures but mostly by the absolutely fantastic view.

'Wow,' said Jim. 'I love this. Your view is way better than ours. I bet you have a great time – sitting here with your binoculars and a G&T.'

Colin laughed. 'Well it's great when the weather is like this but not so cosy in the middle of winter when it's blowing a gale and bloody freezing.'

Saskia and Sally were straight into girly talk, complimenting each other on their hair and clothes and bemoaning the lack of classy clothes shops in the area.

Colin fixed the drinks and he and Jim looked out to sea.

'Sas says you've been looking after her at Seawatch. She really enjoys it and I'm pleased she's got into it – it gives her a new interest and she seems to be getting a lot more fun from coming out on the boat now.'

Jim nodded. 'Yeah, she's slotted in well and she's definitely enthusiastic. She's picking up stuff fast and getting into the training papers.'

'Yeah, she quizzes me on all sorts of stuff and she absolutely amazed me the other day. We anchored for lunch and she only did a three-point fix and showed me where we were on the chart. I was absolutely gobsmacked – I didn't even know she knew what a three-point fix was.'

Jim laughed. 'That's good – I don't think she'll be a trainee for long. I'd bet she'll be a fully-fledged watchkeeper by the winter.'

Saskia said 'Would you all like to come through. I hope you don't mind but we're eating in the kitchen/diner. We have got a dining room but we use it as our study and we've got the computer and printer and loads of paperwork all over the dining table.'

The kitchen/diner was spacious and Saskia served the starters while Colin poured the wine. Crayfish salad and Viognier.

Saskia sipped her wine. 'So I hear you two haven't been married all that long – any previous marriages?'

Sally looked surprised. 'No – I guess that's pretty unusual at our age. But Jim was wedded to his business and I was either acting or looking for acting work. I think we both spent too much time working and not enough time socialising. My mum and dad had been asking me all my life when I was going to settle down and start a family. But you two were late starters as well weren't you?'

Colin laughed. 'We were both married to the IT industry. Lots of travel – too much travel. Not enough time for fun, so now we want to make up for that.'

Jim put down his knife and fork. 'Sounds like all that travel should have given you the opportunity for some fun?'

Saskia said, 'It was fun to start with but then as you get older the novelty wears off. I used to have weeks where I was in a different hotel every night. You get up to use the bathroom in the middle of the night and walk into the wall because you're headed for where the bathroom was the previous night.'

Sally laughed. 'Did that really happen?'

'Oh yeah, several times. For most of my career the company was doing well and they looked after you really well – good salary package, car and club class travel. Then profits started to slide as the industry evolved and suddenly it was economy class. Long haul flights to San Francisco are no fun at all when you're in economy with your knees under your bloody chin.'

Sally was interested. 'That all sounds very different to my life. When you were staying in fancy hotels I was stuck in disgusting cheap B&Bs.'

Saskia started clearing the plates. 'Jim says you were an actress and then you became an author.'

'Yes, well that makes it sound a bit grander than it really was. I was mainly a bit-part actress and then I ended up indie-publishing some novels.'

Colin topped up everyone's glasses. 'What sort of novels?'

'Oh, a series of stories about a private detective who gets involved in the theatre world. They didn't sell in huge numbers but they were reasonably successful. That's how I first met Jim. I gave a talk at the Felixstowe book festival and he was in the audience.'

Jim laughed. 'Yeah, I was already a fan and I queued up to get my book signed.'

Sally giggled. 'It wasn't a very long queue.'

Saskia brought in the main course – beef bourguignon with a selection of veggies. Colin opened the bottle of Cote du Rhone that they'd brought and he and Jim switched to red while the girls opted to stay on white for now.

Jim sipped his wine. 'I meant to bring you a yachting magazine Colin – somebody gave it to me at the golf club – must have thought I was still one of you lot. But I forgot it – bloody typical – bringing three things is too much for my brain to cope with. It's amazing I remembered the flowers and the wine. Do you have a problem remembering stuff?'

Colin grimaced. 'I can't remember anything these days. It's pathetic – I'm 65 years old and I can't remember anything. I forget my pin numbers, the burglar alarm code, our wedding anniversary, everything. If you ever see me with a black eye you'll know I've forgotten Sas' birthday. If all the bills weren't on direct debit we'd probably have our gas and electric cut off. Oh no – that's not right – we haven't even got a bloody gas supply – forgot that too.'

Jim laughed. 'They say it's because we've got too many distractions these days. Our mums and dads didn't talk about forgetting stuff because they didn't spend half their lives on iPads and mobile phones. I guess they just didn't have much to think about. Nobody was worried about their social media presence in those days. Life was so much simpler – and probably better. Anyway, you were saying that Sal and me were late starters on the marriage front but I hear you were too.'

Colin nodded. 'Yeah, it's unusual isn't it? Two childless couples getting together relatively late in life. If we were typical we would probably have had at least a couple of previous partners and a string of kids.'

Jim laughed. 'It's saved us all some money.'

Sally said, 'Typical – he's always thinking of the financial angle.'

Saskia chipped in. 'You've obviously done alright for yourselves – living in one of those huge places near the golf club. That was a huge house to move into when you were single Jim.'

He put down his knife and fork. 'Well it's not exactly a mansion but I did want a pool. I spent ages trying to find something smaller but there aren't any small houses around that have a pool. At first I did think it was a bit daft having rooms I hardly ever used but since I got together with Sal we seemed to have spread out a bit. The place seems more sort of lived in now.'

Colin refilled all the glasses again. 'It seems like Felixstowe suits all of us but it's not everyone's cup of tea. The seafront has improved a lot in the last couple of years with the new pier and gardens. It's a shame that the town looks so tired – quite a few boarded-up shops now.'

Sally nodded. 'I think it's like most high streets these days – getting killed off by the online world. I even miss M&S now that's gone – despite me always moaning about them. Somehow the posher places like Aldeburgh and Southwold don't really do it for us.'

Colin agreed. 'I think it's because we're into boats. We've stayed in the Wentworth at Aldeburgh a couple of times. Paid extra for a room with a sea view and then you realise there isn't actually anything to see most of the time. Apart from the odd fishing boat. I like to see container ships, ferries, dredgers, yachts, tugs, pilot boats – all the things that make for a proper working port.'

He looked at Jim. 'If you had a Seawatch lookout station at Aldeburgh you'd never be able to stay awake.'

Jim laughed. 'Yeah, I'm like you. I like to see the sea busy. The beef is lovely Saskia, done to perfection. Do you like cooking?'

She smiled, 'Thanks – yes, I suppose I do but I prefer eating out. I don't like all the mess I make in the kitchen – all the washing up – even if most of it does go in the dishwasher.'

Sally finished everything on her plate. 'Yes, that was great. I'll have to cook for you next time but I've obviously got a lot to live up to.'

Saskia cleared the plates while Colin topped up everyone's glass again.

She said 'Hope you've all got room for dessert. It's just strawberries and cream, or ice cream if you like.'

Jim smiled. 'Sounds great to me – I'll have mine with ice cream please. I don't think you need to cook tomorrow Sal.'

'No – it's rations for you the rest of the week.'

Colin glanced at his iPad. 'Looks like getting a lot warmer this week. Good boating weather.'

Jim nodded. 'Might be a bit too warm for much golf but I'll probably play early morning before it starts getting uncomfortable. When you come to ours it might be a good idea if we had lunch instead of dinner and then we could all have a swim.'

He closed his eyes momentarily and pictured the lovely Saskia in a bikini. He thought he'd have to try to hold his paunch in to stop his roll of fat sagging over his trunks.

Colin cleared all the plates and suggested they all move back into the lounge. He asked if anyone fancied a brandy or a liqueur. The girls wanted to stay on the wine but both Jim and Colin opted for brandies with coffee.

By now everyone had that nice glow you feel after a good meal washed down with some good wine.

It was still light and there were plenty of people strolling along the prom. Two ships in the anchorage switched their lights on and a pilot boat headed out to the next unseen container ship which would need ushering in.

Saskia sat next to Sally on the sofa. 'So what have you got planned this week then?'

Sally thought. 'I need to do a few jobs around the house and I'll go into Ipswich to do a bit of shopping. We always eat out a couple of times and do some walking. On Wednesday night I'm going to the Am Dram society get-together – it will be my first time.'

'That should be good – they'll be thrilled to get a professional joining them.'

Sally smiled. 'Oh, I'm not going to tell them anything about my past – I don't want to create any expectations that I have trouble living up to. I wasn't exactly a star you know.'

'I bet you're being modest. If you were making a living then you must have been good.'

Sally shook her head. 'I just got by, thanks to regular hand-outs from Mum and Dad. The family home was always my base so I never had to pay out for rent or a mortgage. No – if it hadn't been for them I'd have had to get a proper job.'

Everyone continued chatting until long after dark and then Jim and Sally said they'd have to head home. They said their thank-yous and everyone agreed it had been a good night.

They walked home hand-in-hand and chatted.

'So what did you think to them?' asked Jim.

'Yeah – nice couple, lovely meal. I like their place – fantastic views. You and Saskia seem to get on well.'

'Yes, she's easy to get on with and it's nice that joining Seawatch has made her more enthusiastic about getting out on the boat with Colin.'

'Does she actually drive the boat herself?'

'Yeah – but there's not much to it when they're just using the engine. It's just a steering wheel and throttle. She doesn't get involved with the sails because she doesn't like getting out of the river. Colin only bothers to put the canvas up if he takes her past Landguard and out to sea.'

'Do you think she's pretty?'

'I guess so – she seems to have kept herself in good shape.'

'Does that imply I haven't?'

Jim looked at her warily. 'Not at all – you don't need to be defensive. Both of you are fine looking women.'

'You certainly like her legs – you were looking at them enough.'

He sighed. 'Don't let's spoil a nice evening Sal.'

She looked straight ahead. 'I'm not going to – just stating a fact. No – it was nice and I like both of them. It's a good idea inviting them round for lunch and a swim, but if she wears a bikini just make sure your tongue doesn't hang out.'

Chapter 14

The good thing about catching the night ferry was that Jim and Sally had all day to pack and get ready. The only problem was that although the Stena left from Harwich, just across the water from Felixstowe, they had a thirty mile drive around the river to get there.

They always used the same routine when crossing on the Stena. Although the ship didn't leave until nearly 11pm they started boarding about 8.30. They would drive on, dump their overnight bag in the cabin and be sat in the restaurant by 9.

The holiday could then begin with a good three course dinner and a bottle of wine and they were usually in bed by the time the ship sailed. Jim just loved these holidays – no airports, pleasant drives, nice hotels, good food and drink and the chance to really enjoy time with Sally. Much as he loved her and spent a large part of every day with her it seemed different. No visitors or phone calls – just the two of them.

The only slight downer was the early morning arrival at the Hook of Holland. It was always a rush to get up, shower and eat breakfast before the announcement came over the tannoy that all drivers should head down to the car decks.

Sally would have been happy to have a bit more sleep and skip breakfast but Jim felt he really needed it before tackling a long day's driving. They always made the crossing on a Saturday night so that they were driving off the ship and around the outskirts of Rotterdam early on Sunday, when there was little or no traffic to contend with.

He would have liked to share the driving but Sally was adamant she couldn't drive on the 'wrong' side of the road. They did this holiday every year – visiting various different cities around Europe. This time it was going to be two nights in Hannover, three in Berlin, three in Prague, an overnight stop in Frankfurt and finally two nights in Brussels before heading back on the ferry.

This first leg would be about 300 miles and with a couple of good long breaks and some rapid progress on the autobahn it was an easy journey of between six and seven hours.

The early Sunday traffic was indeed predictably light and the Merc comfortably swallowed up the miles. They were soon through Holland and on to the faster pace of the autobahn. Jim set the cruise control at 80mph but wasn't surprised to see lots of cars zooming past, going way over a ton.

Sally didn't like him driving fast but he always maintained it was dangerous to drive at less than 80 on the autobahn as you were just getting in everyone's way. When she dozed off he clicked the cruise control up to 90.

They stopped twice at service stations to have a coffee, use the toilet and stretch their legs. They arrived at the hotel on the outskirts of Hannover mid-afternoon. Jim had booked a hotel on the outskirts, which was next to a tram stop, giving easy access into the city centre.

He walked up to the pretty girl at the reception desk and said,

'Guten abend, mein name ist Herr Ellis. Ich habe rezervace fur zwci nocht.'

She smiled condescendingly and said. 'Good afternoon Mr. Ellis – can you please complete the registration card.'

He grinned. It seemed pointless trying to learn a foreign language these days as just about everywhere you went people only wanted to practice their English on you. He mused that we were lucky - our native language is the most useful language on earth. Everyone else seemed to have a much greater incentive to learn English than we had to learn anything else.

Once in the room they dumped their bags, made coffee and put their feet up. They both felt too tired to go into the city and agreed they would eat dinner in the hotel and then have a full day sightseeing the following day.

The hotel was typically Germanic – clean, modern, everything you need – but a bit soulless. They had G&Ts in the bar, followed by a big two course dinner washed down with a bottle of cabernet sauvignon. They were in bed before ten, they snuggled up together and slept like proverbial babies.

They opened the curtains on to a bright sunny day. Jim put on shorts and a polo shirt while Sally opted for a summery shirt and three-quarter length trousers. After a hearty breakfast they got the tram into the city. Neither of them had ever been to Hannover before so they followed their usual routine in a new city and got on the hop on – hop off sightseeing bus. A one hour tour gave them an overview of what was where and they worked out what they wanted to do and see.

When staying in hotels they always ate a huge breakfast and a big dinner and had nothing in between. They strolled around the Herrenhaeuser Gardens – a mix of baroque, botanical and English styles. They went in the Altes Rathaus – the city hall, which had been flattened in WW2 but was now beautifully restored.

They had coffees at a pavement café, spent an hour wandering round the aquarium and were back at the hotel by the end of the afternoon.

Sally phoned her Mum while Jim used his iPad to find out what was going on in the world. Over dinner Jim got the maps out and worked out their route to Berlin the following day. Sally studied the Berlin guide book and quizzed Jim on just what they would be able to do and see.

Berlin was his favourite city and he had been there a number of times on business and for pleasure. He first went there when the wall was still in place and would never forget the incredible contrast between east and west. He was there on a business conference and on a free day he went over to the east with a colleague.

They crossed at Checkpoint Charlie and the difference was breath-taking. Affluent well-dressed people, Mercs and BMWs on one side and dowdy, downtrodden looking people and Trabants on the other. Instead of the sumptuous emporia in the west stocking everything anyone could possible want there were scruffy shops displaying soap powder and tins of beans in the window.

They found the poshest restaurant they could find for lunch which was faded, poorly lit and served up a disgusting meal for a pittance. The sheer dreadfulness of East Berlin was somehow fascinating in its awfulness. It seemed almost ghoulish to be enjoying seeing the dark side of the world knowing that you would be back to luxury by evening.

He thought back to when they'd arrived at the airport earlier in the week. The taxi driver had quipped. 'Why does the sun have a smile on its face in the morning?'

Jim had smiled politely and shrugged his shoulders.

'Because it knows it will be in the west by the end of the day.'

He could see the sun's point of view.

Sally had never been there before so Jim decided to splash out and really show off his favourite place. He had booked them into a smart five star hotel on the Kurfurstendamm, in the very centre of the city. Kurfurstendamm was often referred to as Berlin's equivalent to the Champs Elysee – lots of smart hotels, restaurants and upmarket shops.

The traffic was heavy and Jim was happy to get the car into the hotel's underground car park. They settled into the room and went for a stroll. He had always thought that you could really feel the history of the city everywhere you went – probably because so much of it was recent. So much happened there in the two world wars and then the images of the wall coming down were familiar to people the world over.

Sally was fascinated by the Kaiser Wilhelm church – bombed in 1943 and its damaged appearance left as a perpetual reminder of the horrors of war. He explained that the locals called it der hohle Zahn – the hollow tooth.

She loved KaDeWe – Berlin's equivalent to Harrods – and Jim lashed out on two glasses of ridiculously expensive champagne in the bar on the top floor. They toasted their love for each other like lovestruck teenagers.

Back at the hotel they had their usual G&Ts in the bar before finding a cosy little restaurant for dinner. Sally decided she loved the place just as much as Jim did and they couldn't have been happier.

Over a particularly good bottle of Bordeaux Jim outlined the plans for the following day.

'I'm going to take you to my favourite museum.'

Sally smiled politely. 'Are you sure – you know I'm not really a fan of museums.'

'You will be of this one. It's the Checkpoint Charlie museum – loads of exhibits showing the escapes from east to west over the years that the wall was in place. It's the only museum I've ever been to where I've read all the text that goes with the exhibits and it's very hands on. Some of the stories of failed attempts are really tragic but mostly they're really uplifting tales of success and freedom.'

'Okay, sounds good. What are we doing after that?'

'Thought we'd do some of the main sights – the Reichstag, Brandenburg gate, stroll down Unter den Linden and relax in the Tiergarten – that's a beautiful park.'

'I can remember seeing a film once that showed people parading down Unter den Linden. It looked really posh.'

'Yeah, it was. Before the wall went up it really was The place to go – the ladies loved to walk down there in their Sunday best. It was a poseurs paradise.'

Jim settled the bill and they strolled back to the hotel.

'Fancy a nightcap before we hit the sack.'

Sally chuckled. 'Not sure, maybe you just want to take advantage of me.'

'Well I do – that's the idea.'

They both giggled and half an hour later they were both enjoying a perfect end to a super day.

As predicted Sally did indeed love the museum and everything else about Berlin. When they left the city to head for Prague Sally grabbed Jim's hand.

'Thanks for that darling – it was fantastic. Why haven't I been to Berlin before? It's a terrific place.'

'Yeah, it is and it's sort of become extra cool since the wall came down. It's been restored as the German capital and it's just got so much character – the place is so alive.'

'So now we're headed somewhere else I've never been.'

'Oh you'll love Prague too – it's very different to Berlin but It's got lots of history and masses of wonderful old buildings – and they're all in fantastic condition. It's a lot less expensive than

Germany so I've booked us a suite at the hotel. That works out a lot cheaper than a standard room in most European cities.'

'We're staying at a hotel in Mala Strana – that means the lesser town – it's on the other side of the Vltava river from the main part of the city. Over the years it's become the cool arty side – it's near the cathedral and has loads of trendy restaurants and bars.'

On arrival Jim parked the car in another underground car park. They carried their bags up to Reception and Jim made another attempt to impress Sally.

He smiled at the very smart young guy behind the desk.

'Dobry den – jak se mate?'

'I'm very well thank you sir – I assume you are Mr. and Mrs. Ellis?'

Jim grinned – another city where his attempts to learn a few basic phrases proved absolutely futile.

They signed in and the young man picked up their cases and led them up to their suite. It was on a corner of the top floor, with huge panoramic windows on two sides. One window looked out to the castle and the other to the Charles bridge, spanning the river.

'Oh Jim, this is fantastic – what a beautiful place.'

They showered and changed and headed out for a stroll in the warm evening air.

'We're not cating posh tonight Sal. The last time I was here was for a conference and some of the local guys took me to their favourite pub. The food was fantastic and the atmosphere was great, with live music.'

'Sounds good to me. I might get a dance?'

'Maybe – if this old boy can still manage it.'

The pub was already busy and a trio were belting out some good old soft rock numbers.

Sally was all smiles. 'Oh I like this. Can I be unladylike and have a beer?'

Jim laughed. 'Of course, what else – Czech beer is reckoned to be the best in the world.'

He ordered two draught Staropramen - which came in big tankards.

'One thing you need to know Sal. This is a typical Czech pub and so if you empty your glass the barman will assume you want the same again and he'll bring you another one.'

'Wow – sounds good to me. But what happens when I've had enough?'

'When you are on your last drink you leave a little in the glass until we're ready to go. Then you drain the glass, we stand up, go to the bar and settle our bill.'

'That's fantastic, no queueing and trying to catch the barman's eye then?'

'No. It works well but we can eat here as well if you like. I had a fantastic meal here before – a local speciality. It was like a small cottage loaf with the middle hollowed out and it was filled with beef goulash.'

'Sounds great to me – with a glass of red please.'

So they had their typical Czech cuisine, quite a lot more red wine, a couple of dances and walked unsteadily back to the hotel.

As they walked into the room Sal said 'can I just brush my teeth before we do anything else?'

Jim gave her his naughty boy smile, pushed her on the bed and said, 'No chance, that will have to wait.'

The following day they had their usual big breakfast and then spent the day trekking around all the main tourist attractions of Prague. Sally loved the castle and the old town square, where they sat in the sunshine drinking coffee while watching the world go by. They took a boat trip along the river and strolled around the little streets of Mala Strana.

The drive back across Germany to Brussels was too long to comfortably do it in one day and so they had an overnight stop in a hotel on the outskirts of Frankfurt.

They had both been to Brussels before and had done the tourist's favourite sightseeing spots and so they just relaxed, ate and drank and wandered around the city.

That evening Jim checked his phone. The usual junk emails and just one new text. 'Hi Jim, hope you're both having a fantastic holiday. I'm missing you so I booked to be on watch with you next Saturday. Take care. Love Sas x.'

He was surprised by the kiss but figured that seemed to be the norm now. You get a x from people you've never met.

The journey back on the ferry went to plan and they arrived home late at night.

'Well Jimbo, that was fantastic – a super holiday. Thanks for all that driving and getting us home safe and sound.'

Jim grinned. 'Glad you liked it. I'm sure I've put on loads of weight though. Can we have beans on toast tomorrow?'

'Oh, I was going to cook you a big thank-you dinner.'

'Let's pass on that. There is another way you can thank me though.'

They both had a long lie-in the next morning.

Chapter 15

While Jim was away on holiday Saskia put herself down for a watch with Mike Ford.

When they'd set everything up and there was a lull in proceedings Mike put down his binoculars.

'I bet Jim and Sally are having a fine old time. They love their driving holidays.'

Saskia nodded. 'Yeah, I wish they had a spare seat for me. Sounds like they go to really nice places and I expect they stay in some fancy hotels'.

Mike laughed. 'I bet they do. Jim's not short of a few bob and he likes the finer things in life.'

'No, I guess he can't be short of money living in one of those big places by the golf club. They must cost a fortune.'

'Well Jim owned the lion's share of a firm in the City and lived in a detached house in Stanmore. I think he found prices dirt cheap when he upped and moved to Felixstowe.'

Saskia was staring vacantly out of the window. 'I wonder how he made all that money.'

Mike smiled. 'Oh, Jim's a clever guy and I guess he was living and working in the right area at the right time and built the business up through the years.'

'He seems very different to Sally. He's a real businessman and she doesn't seem to have done much with her life.'

Mike laughed. 'I think she's a nice lady who really fell on her feet when she met him. They absolutely dote on each other.'

'Do you think so? I wondered if she felt a bit uncomfortable – you know, not contributing anything much wealth wise. Maybe she can't quite believe her luck.'

'I dunno really. I just think they're both nice people and I'm glad things worked out for both of them late in life.'

Saskia looked deep in thought. 'Yeah, it's a bit odd though don't you think? Both of them getting to retirement age and never having been married before – no kids. I know that Colin and me both fit in to that bracket so maybe it's all doubly weird.'

'I really don't know. I expect they've both had various relationships over the years but I guess they never got around to making anything permanent. I guess some people are just like that. When they're working they have enough going on in their lives that they don't feel lonely – they've probably never spent much time on their own.'

She looked puzzled. 'But I don't think Sally was ever that busy. She had big gaps between acting jobs and lived with mum and dad most of her life. What sort of life is that? Why didn't she find herself a husband and have two or three kids?'

Mike laughed. 'I dunno – what is this, the third degree?'

She smiled. 'I'm sorry Mike. It's just that Jim introduced me to Seawatch and I wanted to know a bit more about him.'

Mike looked quizzical. 'Well all I really know is he's a nice guy and I suppose he's quite good looking to the ladies.'

Saskia grinned. 'Yeah, I guess so. I hadn't really thought about that', she said unconvincingly.

Mike laughed. 'Yes – it just hadn't occurred to you.'

She felt her cheeks burning and turned to look at nothing on the radar screen.

'Anyway Saskia – fancy a coffee?'

Jim wandered out to the pool. Sally was sitting on a recliner with papers and a notepad scattered around her.

'What are you doing Sal?'

'Oh this is some stuff I was given at the Am Dram meeting the other night. It's part of the script for a play they're putting on in the autumn.'

'Sounds interesting – are you going to be in it?'

'Maybe – I know the play. It's Absurd Person Singular' - an old Alan Ayckbourn classic.'

'What's it about?'

'Three couples who get together each Christmas and as time goes on their fortunes change. Two of the husbands are successful – one's a bank manager and the other is an architect.

The third husband is a poorly educated jack-the-lad type of tradesman.'

'Go on – what happens?'

'Well the two successful guys initially look down on the tradesman but over the years things change. The bank manager and the architect hit hard times while the other guy goes from strength to strength and makes a ton of money.'

'Good for him.'

'Yes, well - as his fortunes improve he gets more and more confident and the other two go from looking down at him to envying him and he sort of gets the upper hand.'

'I like the sound of it – is it funny?'

'Yeah, it is. It has a brilliant ending where the jack-the-lad type makes everyone play party games. He's really loving it while the others are squirming with embarrassment and you realise he is humiliating them and getting his revenge.'

'Good stuff – and where would you fit in?'

'Well, they asked me if I'd think about playing Jane – the wife of the tradesman type.'

Jim laughed. 'Yeah, I guess you have experience of being married to a jack-the-lad chancer?'

Sally laughed. 'No I don't think so. It's set in the early seventies and it's typically sexist for the time – it focusses on the fortunes of the men while all three wives are just wives.'

'Is Jane nice?'

'Yeah, I like her. She's up and down and gets a bit bossy at times but I think it might be a fun part.'

'Good for you – go for it. I'll definitely come. Where will it be on?'

'Oh a variety of local venues over a two week period.'

'I'm just going to make another coffee and then I'm golfing. What are you doing?'

'Pam and Anne are coming over for coffee and a swim.'

'Okay, lots of girly talk then.'

'Yeah, you'll be well out of it. Enjoy your golf.'

Colin joined his wife on the balcony. 'How was Seawatch today then?'

'Good. I was on with Mike Ford. You probably know him from the yacht club.'

'Oh yeah, I do. He's a nice guy – got a tidy little sloop. He knows his stuff Mike – I think he's been around the water most of his life.'

'He certainly knows a lot more than me and he seems easy going.'

'Who do you like being on with most?'

'Everyone has been fine. Steve Tomlinson is a nice guy and of course Jim is good company.'

'Yeah, I'm looking forward to seeing their place. Weren't they going to invite us for lunch?'

'I'm on with Jim again next week so he'll probably ask us then.'

It was the following Tuesday afternoon when they next met up in the lookout. It was an overcast but breezy day and Colin was out in Tulip.

'Is Colin getting the canvas up today?'

'Yes, he's intending to so I'll keep an eye out for him. He's got a mate with him today.'

Jim logged a big OOCL container ship on the way out and Saskia studied the CCTV.

'There's a woman in a rubber ring down near the Dip. She doesn't look too confident – bet she can't swim.'

'Better keep an eye on her then – the tide's going out.'

'So you both enjoyed the holiday then?'

'Yeah, we did. Probably ate and drank too much but then that's what holidays are for. Sally loved Berlin and Prague most – she'd never been to either.'

'Lots of sightseeing?'

'Yeah, all the usual touristy things that most people do.'

'Lots of lovely meals in expensive restaurants I bet?'

'Well yes but one night I took her to a pub in Prague I'd been to before. It was dirt cheap but good beer, local cuisine and live music – that was fun.'

'Did you dance?'

'Yeah we had a jig. I can only manage a bit of dad dancing these days mind you.'

'How does Sally handle all that time in the car – doesn't she get bored?'

'No, she seems okay. Studies the maps, looks at guide books and dozes. She takes various pillows and cushions so she can get really comfortable.'

'How about you? How do you handle all those miles?'

'Oh I like it. I'd much rather drive than be a passenger.'

'Oh look, there's Tulip. He's going well in this breeze – got both sails up. Could I call him on the radio?'

'Yeah sure. You shouldn't really as you haven't got your radio licence yet but I won't tell if you don't.'

She grinned and picked the mic up.

'Yacht Tulip, Yacht Tulip this is Felixstowe Seawatch, Felixstowe Seawatch. Radio check. Over.'

'Felixstowe Seawatch this is Yacht Tulip, you are loud and clear and it's lovely to be talking to my favourite watchkeeper.'

'Hi darling – how are you getting on out there?'

'Felixstowe Seawatch this is Yacht Tulip – can you please use correct radio procedure. Over.'

'Yacht Tulip this is Felixstowe Seawatch. Oops sorry. Over.'

'Felixstowe Seawatch this is Yacht Tulip. Better tighten up Sas or Jim will be putting you over his knee. Have a good watch, see you later. Out.'

She put the mic back and laughed. 'That would be fun.'

'What would?'

'You putting me over your knee – I think I'd like that.'

Jim grinned. He suspected she wasn't joking.

'Actually, you could do anything up here. It's so private. I wonder if there's ever been anything naughty going on between watchkeepers.'

Jim laughed. 'I doubt it – there are very few women watchkeepers.'

'Doesn't have to be a man and a woman these days!'

'No, I guess not. But it wouldn't look good if Seawatch missed an incident because the watchkeepers were otherwise engaged.'

She chuckled. 'What a thought though. You could lock this door and get up to absolutely anything – only the two people on watch would know.'

Jim decided it was time to change topic. 'Do you want to practice some plotting. I could give you a scenario where you'd have to imagine somebody was in trouble and you'd have to plot their position and work out what the tidal stream was doing. We could simulate a man overboard situation.'

She sighed. 'Okay, if you say so. It's not as much fun as if you were to lock the door and bend me over the chart table but I suppose it is more professional.'

He never knew when she was kidding.

Chapter 16

It was another couple of weeks when Saskia and Colin took up the lunch invitation.

Sally called Saskia that morning. 'Hi Saskia – looks like we've got a hot day for it. Why don't you both come round about 11'ish. Bring your swimming gear and you can both have a swim before lunch. We're just having salad by the pool, nothing fancy.'

'Okay Sally – sounds great. We're both looking forward to it. See you later.'

They strolled down in the hot summer sunshine with flowers for Sally and a cold bottle of New Zealand Sauvignon blanc.

Colin spotted the house first. 'Bloody hell Sas – look at the size of it. I bet you could fit our place in their lounge.'

Saskia smiled. 'If we win the lottery this is the sort of place I'd like. Nice cars too, his and hers Mercs.'

Jim answered the doorbell. 'Hi you two – you're looking nice and summery.'

Saskia was wearing a cool pink top over white knee length shorts, with strappy sandals. Colin had on a red and white striped yachting shirt over beige knee length shorts.

Jim was looking ready for the pool. He was wearing the pale green casual shirt, which Sally always said looked really good on him, over the top of his swimming trunks.

He led them straight through the house to the pool.

'The changing room is over there when you need it and there's a shower in there.'

'Great' said Colin. 'I'm really hot and sweaty already – I don't want to pollute your pool.'

Saskia looked around at the classy poolside furniture – recliners, chairs, one big table with eight chairs and several small tables for drinks and bits and pieces. 'This is gorgeous – and such a big pool. I love your garden – all those lovely shrubs and the grass looks in great condition.'

Jim smiled. 'I can't take any credit for that – it's all down to Graham, the gardener. I like to enjoy time in the garden but I just don't want to do any work in it. Sal likes to plant stuff and she'll often work with Graham, but I'm usually skiving on the golf course while they do it.'

Sally appeared looking at her best in a pale blue and white striped cotton shirt, well cut beige three quarter length trousers and gold coloured flip flops.

Colin kissed her on the cheek. 'Hi Sally – you look great.'

Saskia looked her up and down before kissing. 'Thanks so much for inviting us – I've really been looking forward to this. I love the pool and the garden – can I be cheeky and ask for a tour of the house?'

'Of course. Jim can you fix some drinks first and then while I get lunch organised you can show Saskia around.'

Predictably Saskia was bowled over by the house. The lounge and dining room were both huge with expensive looking Italian light wood furniture and thick rugs on a wood floor. She thought the kitchen was bigger and better equipped than most kitchens found in restaurants. There were his and hers studies on the ground floor and six bedrooms above. The master bedroom had an en-suite bathroom and a big walk-in dressing room. One other bedroom had an en-suite and a large family bathroom serviced the others.

'This is amazing Jim – I'm so envious.'

'Well your place is lovely and you've got a better view.'

'We might have a view but you've got about ten times the space we have and you've got everything just so – super furniture.'

When they returned to the pool Colin was already swimming. He surfaced and shook the water from his eyes.

'It's lovely in here Sas – get your gear off.'

She disappeared into the changing room and came out ten minutes later in a one- piece swimsuit. Jim registered that she wasn't showing any fat at all.

'Can I dive in Jim or don't the health and safety regs allow that?'

He laughed. 'I always dive in because I'm a wuss when I go down the steps – it takes me ages to get used to the water at first. It doesn't seem a problem when you dive in – but it'll mess your hair up.'

She duly dived in and was immediately doing an impressive crawl. Jim had expected a girly breast stroke with head held high.

Jim dived in, did a length underwater and then several lengths crawl before climbing up the steps.

He dried himself with a big beach towel. 'I'll refill the glasses and then help Sal get the food out.'

They put plates and cutlery on the big table and then brought a big platter of smoked salmon, pots of crab, a huge bowl of mixed salad and all sorts of dressings. 'Help yourselves everyone.'

Sally was pleased to see everyone loading their plates and then having seconds. They quickly demolished the bottle of Sauvignon that Colin and Saskia had brought and then Jim fetched another and by mid-afternoon they were on the third.

Dessert had been fresh fruit salad and cream. The combination of good food, good wine and the hot sun put everyone at ease and they all laid on recliners and chatted.

Saskia pushed her sunglasses on to the top of her head and looked at Sally. 'Super lunch Sal – thanks. Jim was telling me you are going to be in a play.'

Sally laughed. 'Oh, just something the local Am Dram society are putting on.'

'Do they know they've got a professional in their midst?'

'Oh I'm not telling anyone I used to do it for a living. They'd expect me to be half decent.'

'I bet you're more than half decent – you'll be a knockout. I can't wait to see it.'

'Don't expect too much – you might be wanting your money back.'

'What sort of roles did you used to play?'

'Oh, all sorts. Wives, mistresses, teachers, secretaries, shop girls – I've been in the army, navy and air force. Posh roles, tarty roles, bimbo roles. You name it.'

'You must be really talented to be so diverse.'

'Oh I was never top of the bill in anything.'

'So that paid a living?'

'Sort of, but if it wasn't for mum and dad I'd have starved.'

'A good looking girl like you – I wonder why you weren't snapped up. Didn't you ever meet the right man before Jim?'

'Oh I had lots of relationships – like everyone. Lots of failed relationships to be honest – men who turned out to be weird, controlling, married, crooked and one who got turned on by beating the living daylights out of me.'

'Oh Sal – how horrible.'

She laughed. 'Well, I generalise – they weren't all like that. Some of them were really nice and it was probably my fault it didn't come to anything.'

Saskia spread her arms wide. 'So you didn't really shine at anything but you ended up with all this. You certainly landed on your feet when you met Jim. Wish I'd got there first.'

Three pairs of eyes turned on Saskia. Sally looked bloody cross, Colin looked furious and Jim just looked gobsmacked.

Saskia laughed. 'Joke, everyone.'

But nobody found it funny and the mood was killed. Not long after Colin said they'd have to make a move – he thanked Sally and Jim for a lovely lunch and swim.

As soon as they were out of earshot Colin glared at her.

'So what the bloody hell was that about? They give us a lovely day, they couldn't have been nicer and then you decide to totally rubbish Sal. Where did that come from? What have you got against her?'

'I haven't got anything against her – I'd just had a bit too much vino and my mouth ran away with me. It was harmless.'

'No, it wasn't harmless. It was tactless – savage – downright bloody nasty. You really upset her.'

'I'll send her some flowers with an apology note.'

'That's the least you can do. We won't be getting invited there again. And how do you I think felt when you said you wished you'd met him first. Doesn't do a lot for me does it?'

'Oh lighten up for god's sake. It was just one stupid remark. I suppose I'll be in the doghouse for days now.'

'You deserve to be.'

Not another word was said between them for the rest of the day.

First thing the following morning Saskia phoned the local florist and ordered a large hand-tied bouquet to be delivered to Sally ASAP with a card bearing the message.

'To Sally & Jim. Thanks so much for a wonderful day. I'm afraid the wine went to my head and I said something stupid which I am truly sorry for. Please forgive me. Love Sas xxx'

Jim felt more awkward than angry.

'I'm so sorry Sal. I don't know why the hell she said that – maybe it was just the wine talking.'

'Well, she's not coming here again. What a bloody cheek.'

'Yeah, it was totally out of order. I can't believe she said that.'

'Maybe she's just stupid – maybe she was simply pissed – or maybe she's got designs on my husband.'

'Oh Sal, don't say that. It just came out of nowhere – she's been fine when I do watches with her. She hasn't said anything out of order – she's just been a typical new watchkeeper.'

'Well I'm not keen on you doing more watches with her. If she's like that when her husband is around I dread to think what she might do when there's just the two of you alone in the lookout.'

'I've got a couple more watches booked with her in the next month but if there's any sort of problem I promise I won't book myself for any more watches that she's already down for. The problem is if she puts herself down for a watch that I'm already booked for.'

131

'If there's any hint of a problem you will just have to tell her you don't want to be on with her.'

'That would be awkward Sal.'

'It might be awkward but I'm telling you Jim, that's what you'll have to do.'

Chapter 17

It was turning into a long hot summer. There had been very little rain for months and Jim was having to top up the pool with the hose every day.

Some days golf was turning out to be really tiring. The baked fairways were allowing the ball to run much further but very often this meant balls running into gorse bushes and bunkers.

Sally was getting busy with her Am Dram role and he was pleased to see her being so enthusiastic about it.

One warm evening Jim attended a Seawatch training session at the local library. He got there early and spread some papers out on the vacant chair next to him. Just as the session was about to start Saskia appeared, picked up his papers, sat down and said 'got room for a little one?'

'Oh, hi Saskia. Haven't seen you for a while – how are you?'

She giggled. 'I've been keeping a low profile after disgracing myself.'

'Oh don't worry about it. What's done is done.'

'No, I'm sorry Jim. It was inexcusable – just the booze talking on a hot day.'

The session started and for the next hour and a half they were immersed in a discussion about buoyage and radio procedures.

Coffee was served and Saskia looked at him enquiringly.

'If I invited you and Sal over to ours again do you think she'd come?'

'I don't know Sas. Might be best to let things settle for a while.'

'I've really buggered things up haven't I? I thought we were getting on so well when we did watches together and I wanted the four of us to develop a friendship.'

'I'm sure we can but let's take it easy for now.'

'Okay Jim. Did you come by car tonight?'

'Yeah, I was lazy.'

'I walked as it was such a nice evening but now it's getting dark I don't fancy walking home on my own – don't suppose you'd give me a lift?'

He didn't want to but couldn't think how he could say no and it was only a five minute drive.

They made polite small talk and he stopped the car at the back of her apartment block.

She leaned toward him. 'Thanks Jim – and no hard feelings eh?'

He grinned, 'no, goodnight Sas.'

She leaned further towards him and kissed him on the cheek. With a wicked smile on her face she put her hand between his legs.

'Oh, fancy that, maybe you have got a hard feeling.'

And she was out of the car and walking quickly toward the lift without a backwards glance.

Jim sat there for a while – finding it difficult to believe what had just happened. He drove on to the seafront and parked for a good ten minutes before he felt able to continue the drive home.

He parked the car and found Sally busy in the kitchen.

'Hi Sal. Had a good evening?'

'Yeah, we ran through most of the play.'

'And how did it go?'

'Oh, okay. It would be better if everyone read the script properly and learnt their lines though.'

He laughed. 'Bloody amateurs eh!'

'How was your meeting – learn anything new?'

'Yeah, there's always something. It was good – about twenty of us there.'

'Did Saskia go?'

'Yeah, she turned up just as it was starting.'

'Did you speak to her?'

'Yeah, couldn't avoid it – she came and sat next to me.'

'She's got some front that woman – cheeky cow. Did she say anything about the lunch?'

'Only that she'd had too much to drink and she was very sorry.'

'So she bloody should have been.'

'Anyway Sal, when are you having a full dress rehearsal?'

'Next week – it's only three weeks until first night. Some of them have really got a lot of work to do.'

'Is there anything I can do to help?'

'Well, some nights we don't have anyone lined up to sell programmes on the door. Do you fancy putting your name down for a couple of nights?'

'Yeah, no probs. I'm looking forward to it.'

On a hot summer's evening in July Seawatch held their annual dinner at The Julienne, a faded three-star hotel on the edge of Felixstowe. Although other halves could also attend it was usual for just members to be there.

Sally couldn't come anyway as it was the full dress rehearsal for the play and so Jim got a cab there so he could enjoy the evening with a few drinks. There were about thirty people there in all and table placements were posted on a notice board at the entrance to the dining room.

Jim was pleased that although Saskia was there on her own they were on different tables. He was sat on a table with five others, all people he knew. Jim started with a large G&T and the mood was good as everyone started to swap stories. By the end of the crab starter he was already on his second glass of Sauvignon.

The main course was beef so he switched to red and was happily joining in the joke swapping – which was getting progressively bluer as the evening wore on.

Dessert was followed by coffee and brandy and Jim was aware that this was the most he had drunk in a very long time but what the hell – he wasn't driving and he was having a good time.

The draw for the raffle was held and he won a faded looking bag of pot-pourri, which he promptly re-donated. When one of his other tickets won a bottle of wine that was much more acceptable.

People started to drift off but Jim was on his third brandy when Saskia came and sat next to him.

'Hi Jim – had a good evening?'

'Yeah, it was fun. Did you like it?'

She giggled. 'Yeah, had quite a few glasses of the old vino and a bit of a laugh. You look like you've had a few.'

'More than I've had in a long time. Glad I'm not driving and glad I'm not booked for golf in the morning. Fancy another?'

'Yeah, why not.' She smiled and swivelled on her chair so that her leg was touching Jim's. She had a short flowery dress on and killer heels that really showed her legs off to the best effect.

'It's good to see you letting your hair down. You always seem like such a good boy.'

He grinned. 'You mean I'm boring?'

'No, I don't mean that at all. You just always seem very, sort of, together. Can't imagine you ever doing anything wrong.'

'Oh I've done all sorts of things wrong in my time. If I only had a pound...'

'Well we've all done and said stuff we shouldn't have. Broken the speed limit, parked on pavements, avoided paying VAT when we've had the chance. I just don't believe you've done anything really bad – you're not the sort.'

Jim ordered two more brandies and they moved into the lounge as the dining room staff were clearing the tables and just about everyone had left. Her thigh was now pressed against his but he wasn't complaining.

'There's one thing I should never ever have done Sas. It was unforgiveable and I've never told anyone – not even Sal.'

So he unloaded the whole tale about Data Finance. How he used inside knowledge to make a ton of money. How he abused client confidentiality for sheer greed and how that had largely paid for the big house with the pool.

Saskia listened intently. 'That doesn't sound that wicked to me if nobody got hurt.'

'It was wrong Sas. I'm a chartered accountant for god's sake and I drove a proverbial coach and horses through the agreement I had with a valued client. It wasn't right - I'm not proud of it and it bugs me every day.'

'Well I could forgive you, even if Sally couldn't. Anyway Jim it's getting late. Shall we share a cab home?'

It was only a short journey but they both sat in the back and all the way Saskia had her hand between his legs and he had his hand on her knee. When they arrived at hers she kissed him full on the mouth and his hand slid up her thigh as she got out. 'Nite Jim – I enjoyed that. Hope you did too.'

He was relieved that Sally was already in bed and fast asleep when he got home. He fell into a troubled sleep and woke in the morning with a pounding headache.

Sally was already up and he could hear her pottering about in the kitchen. He lay there for a while thinking how bloody stupid he was for letting Sas come on to him as she did. She was a good looking woman but that was no excuse – he must put a stop to it now and get his life back to normal. He couldn't believe just how brazen she was – sexy but dangerous. She was in her late fifties but with good bone structure and a trim figure she looked way more attractive than any of the fat girls in their twenties and thirties he saw waddling around.

More worrying than the daft drunken fumble in the back of the cab was what he had told her. Having kept the lid on his dodgy dealing with Data Finance for so many years he had now confided all to Sas – of all people! He couldn't believe that he had done it – he'd never even told Sal and now he'd blown the whistle to a woman of very dubious morals who'd groped him in the back of a a cab. Stupid, stupid, stupid!

He stumbled down to the kitchen – in urgent need of coffee and paracetamol. Sally was looking as radiant as he was dismal.

'Morning darling. Good night last night?'

'Oh god Sal, that's the most I've drunk for years. I feel absolutely bloody awful.'

'So I take it you enjoyed it? How many of you were there?'

'Oh about thirty.'

'Many people I know?'

'Yeah, quite a few – most of the regulars.'

'Were Saskia and Colin there?'

'Saskia was but fortunately she was on a different table to me.'

'Didn't you talk to her then?'

'Oh, only at the end when we were having coffee. Anyway, how was the rehearsal?'

'It was okay but quite a few cock-ups. Some doughnuts only have a few lines but they can't even remember those. It went on and on – I was knackered when I got home.'

Jim sipped his coffee. 'Thank god I don't have to do anything today. I couldn't play golf if you paid me. Can I help you – got any jobs for me?'

She laughed. 'You don't have to feel guilty about a few drinks. Get something to eat, have a shower and collapse by the pool.'

Friday night was first night for Sally. She was surprised to feel a little bit nervous throughout the day and kept telling herself it was only an am-dram production. It had been well publicised in the local press and was being held in a village hall near Felixstowe. It only held just over 200 and all tickets were sold.

She was pleased when Jim put on his DJ. He might only be the programme seller on the door but he wanted to show her he was fully supportive. The play went well and got lots of laughs – particularly when somebody screwed up.

He was really proud as her acting ability was obviously head and shoulders above the rest of the cast. She might put herself down as a bit-part actress but she looked a real pro in comparison to the others.

It was late by the time they'd all had a glass of wine or a coffee and got changed. On the way home Jim told her how good she'd been and that he was really proud of her.

She kissed him on the cheek. 'And I was proud of my husband – you looked great in your DJ – very handsome.'

He grinned. 'It's getting a bit tight. First time I'd worn it for ages. Definitely need to lose a few pounds.'

Chapter 18

Colin was up early – he wanted a full day on his own on Tulip. He planned to motor down past the docks and Landguard Point, cross the deep-water channel and then put some canvas up and head down to the Frinton area.

Saskia was on watch at Seawatch and he would give her a call on the radio. She was on with Jim and he was uneasy about that because of Sas' moment of madness. He thought the atmosphere might be a bit strained between them. He still couldn't quite believe what came over her that day.

He'd made some sandwiches to eat later and he had a couple of cans of beer in the fridge. He could anchor somewhere quiet, read the paper and do the crossword – should be a nice day.

He arrived at the dock area just as the Stena ferry was departing so hung back to keep well out of her way. There were several yachts around and two tugs heading out, so there was probably a container ship due in soon.

He picked up the mic. 'Felixstowe Seawatch, Felixstowe Seawatch this is Yacht Tulip, Yacht Tulip, requesting radio check. Over.'

He heard his wife's voice. 'Yacht Tulip, Yacht Tulip this is Felixstowe Seawatch, Felixstowe Seawatch. You are loud and clear. Over.'

'Felixstowe Seawatch this is Yacht Tulip. Thanks for that Sas – hope you're having a good watch. Say hello to Jim for me. Over.'

'Yacht Tulip this is Felixstowe Seawatch. Will do – take care and have a good day. See you later. Out.'

The sun was trying to break through and he settled on a course to take him to port and keep him clear of the deep-water channel. The radio came to life again.

'Harwich VTS, Harwich VTS, this is Ocean Traveller, Ocean Traveller. We are now passing 7&8 buoys and getting ready to accept the tugs. Over.'

Harwich VTS controlled all the traffic in and out of the estuary and it was every ship's duty to report to them when nearing the entrance to the Felixstowe and Harwich dock area.

'Ocean Traveller, Ocean Traveller, this Harwich VTS, Harwich VTS. Thanks for that. The Stena Hollandica is now departing but there are no other large vessel movements. Out.'

Colin had looked at the Felixstowe port website before he left home to see what movements were scheduled for the day. The Ocean Traveller was an 'ultra large' container ship, 225,000 tons, and she was headed for the new deep-water berth by the viewing point. It was on its maiden voyage from Shanghai to Felixstowe. There would be lots of cars at the viewing point – people wanting to see this new visitor while they had coffee and cake in the café.

Once he was round Landguard Point he would decide whether to cross the deep-water channel before or after Ocean Traveller had passed in the opposite direction. There were two other yachts also on the way out so he would have to keep an eye out for them as well.

He passed the big radar tower and got his first glimpse of Ocean Traveller. It looked fully loaded so he knew the pilot and the captain would have no view of anything much for at least half a mile ahead of its bow.

Colin wanted a coffee but he would have to wait until he was well clear of the estuary and there was nothing around before he could safely make one. The two tugs both had a line snaking out to the Ocean Traveller and they were getting ready to help it turn the corner into the dock area.

He figured it would be cutting it a bit fine if he crossed the channel ahead of Ocean Traveller and so he would slow down, let it pass and then cross behind it.

Chris and Jackie Norton were having a day out on their yacht Santania. They had risen early in their apartment on the seafront at Shotley and driven down to the marina with everything they needed for a day on the boat. The apartment overlooked the whole Felixstowe and Harwich dock areas. To their left was the River Orwell and to their right was the River Stour.

Chris had always had a soft spot for the area ever since he was a boy seaman at the old naval training establishment HMS Ganges. Ganges had been left semi-derelict after the Navy moved out in the 1970s but now new blocks of apartments were being developed on the old Ganges site.

He and Jackie had been enthusiastic weekend sailors for many years but when they retired and moved to Shotley they had more time. They bought the wooden sloop Santania, which had seen many years service but was still in really good shape. It was only 27 foot long but plenty big enough for what they wanted. With its clean white hull and red and white sails it was a tidy boat. They kept it in the local marina as it was handy, safe and it was protected from the worst of the elements because the marina had a lock.

They transferred their lifejackets, lunch and bits and pieces from the car to the boat. Chris made all his usual checks while Jackie sorted out food and drink in the little galley.

Chris fired up the engine and ten minutes later they were inside the lock watching the water gushing out until it was level with the river. The lock-keeper opened the gates and they were under way, heading towards the sea.

Chris could see the big Stena ferry on its way out, a couple of tugs and two other yachts. He knew from the radio traffic that there was a big container ship on the way in so his plan was to keep well behind the ferry and to port of the deep-water channel. That way he could cross the deep-water channel after the container ship had passed in the opposite direction.

As he approached Landguard Point he could see that one of the other yachts had already crossed the channel safely ahead of the incoming container ship and the other one was just ahead and to port of him. He suspected its plan was similar to his – to cross the channel astern of the container ship.

Jackie was busy in the galley, occasionally popping her head up to see what was happening. Chris called down to her.

'There's just one other sloop to keep an eye on Jackie – just ahead of us and to the left. I think he's got the same plan as us. I won't overtake him – we'll run alongside him, there's room for both of us. Ideally I'd like him a bit further over but I think he's okay.'

James Kirkwood, the Michigan born captain of the Ocean Traveller, was taking it all in. The pilot was happy that they were correctly positioned, doing the right speed and both the tugs were in place.

'So Captain, this is your first time bringing a ship into Felixstowe?'

'Yes, most of my career has been focussed on the States, the Far East and the Middle East. Quite a few European routes but never to Felixstowe. It looks pretty busy.'

The pilot nodded. 'Yes it always is. Felixstowe is the biggest container port in the country and the fourth biggest in Europe. The approaches take a bit of getting used to because the deep-water channel zig zags.'

Kirkwood smiled. 'Yeah, I'm certainly glad you're here.'

'So how is your new ship?'

'Pretty good so far but the usual teething problems – various things don't work. Things got missed during sea trials but that's always the way.'

'Well there's not much wind so this should be a routine approach. There are the usual yachts ahead but they know to keep well away from us.'

'Yeah, they need to because one of things not working is the bow camera, so we can't see anything dead ahead.'

Saskia was keeping a close eye through the big binoculars for Tulip coming into view and before long she said.

'Here he comes – should I give him another call on the radio?'

Jim looked through his binoculars. 'No, probably best to leave it a little while. He's got the Ocean Traveller ahead of him and another yacht near him so he needs to just concentrate for now.'

Colin was aware of the Santania alongside him now and knew they were both just outside the deep-water channel. He looked ahead at the looming container ship and marvelled at the sheer size of it – you never knew quite how ginormous they were until you got this close.

He heard his mobile ringing and realised he'd left it down in the cabin. He'd had an admin problem with renewing his car insurance and had tried to call his broker earlier without success. It had to be sorted or else he'd be driving without cover. He had left a message for him to call back ASAP. He went below, picked up the phone, opened the case and promptly dropped it – more haste, less speed he thought. The phone fell heavily screen down on to the wooden floor. He swore and looked at it to see if it was broken.

It seemed okay and he was answering the call as he made his way back to the wheel. He gasped – the container ship was very close and the other yacht was right alongside him, turning at right angles to cross the bow of Ocean Traveller.

Chris Norton was worried. 'Why doesn't that sod give us more space – surely he can see us.'

Jackie looked over at Tulip. 'I can't even see anyone – there's nobody at the wheel.'

'Bloody hell Jackie. He's getting closer – I'm going to have to cut across the bows of this big bastard. He won't be happy but it's all I can do.'

Jim was watching through his hand-held bins while Saskia watched through the more powerful big bins on the stand.

'Colin's not giving that other yacht much room Sas.'

'No, he's not, why doesn't he turn to port?'

'Can you see him on deck? If anything he's wandering to starboard. They look pretty damn close to that container ship. There's no time to call the Coastguard which is what we probably should do as per the book. I'm going to give him a call directly.'

'Yacht Tulip this is Felixstowe Seawatch. Over.'

There was no response.

'Yacht Tulip this is Felixstowe Seawatch, are you reading me? Over.'

They both said 'oh my god' at exactly the same moment.

Jackie Norton was scared. 'Have we got time to get across his bows?'

'It's either that or we hit that stupid sod.'

As he wrenched the wheel to starboard the way was taken off Santania and she seemed to stall at the critical moment. Jackie screamed as the monstrous bows towered above them and she didn't know anything more. Chris registered Jackie being flung into the air as the ship struck and he heard the dreadful crunching, splintering sound of his boat being smashed to pieces.

Jim was the first to react in the lookout – immediately going into the emergency routine that had been drilled into him by Seawatch. He hit the record button on the tape machine, picked up the phone, called 999 and asked for the Coastguard. His call was answered immediately.

'This is Felixstowe Seawatch. We have just witnessed the Yacht Santania being run down by the container ship Ocean Traveller. The bearing from our lookout station is 185 degrees, distance one nautical mile. The yacht appears to be in pieces – we had been monitoring it and there appeared to be two people visible on board.'

Saskia was shocked. 'Why the hell didn't he turn – why wasn't he at the wheel?'

And so the emergency services swung into action. The Coastguard tasked Harwich RNLI and within seven minutes both the big all-weather lifeboat and the smaller inshore lifeboat left their berth and headed to the scene at top speed. Ocean Traveller didn't appear to have even reduced speed and it was probable that she didn't yet have any idea what had happened.

Then all the radios were alive with traffic. The Coastguard was talking to the Ocean Traveller – Jim was talking to the lifeboats and everyone else in the whole area was reacting to the tragedy that was unfolding.

Jim told Saskia to call station manager Steve Blake and tell him to come to the lookout immediately. She was ashen faced and he had to tell her twice.

The lifeboats were on the scene within a few minutes of being tasked and in no time they were reporting that they had pulled a woman from the water and were continuing to search for any other survivors. Both the ambulance and police force confirmed they would proceed to the RNLI station ready to accept and assist any survivors.

Jim could see that Tulip had turned to port and was heading back in. Saskia was watching through the big binoculars.

'Sas – can you check with Colin that he is okay. The radios are too busy – just give him a quick call on his mobile.'

The lifeboat called to say that the rescued casualty had confirmed that there were only two people on board Santania – Jackie and her husband. Both lifeboats were searching for him and they had been joined by a volunteer rescue boat, a pilot launch and two tugs.

Within minutes the inshore RNLI boat called to say they had found a man and had him onboard – he was unconscious, had a massive head wound and showed no sign of life. Both lifeboats confirmed they were heading straight back to their base to rendezvous with the ambulance and police.

Radio traffic between the Coastguard and Ocean Traveller confirmed that the ship had no idea what had happened. They had been aware of two yachts ahead of them but had lost sight of them before any collision could have taken place. Hitting a yacht wouldn't even have registered - they wouldn't have felt even a slight bump.

For some time Jim was talking to the lifeboats, the Coastguard and Steve Blake. As soon as he could catch his breath he looked at Saskia. 'Did you get Colin?'

'Yeah, he's okay but sounding really panicky. He turned away before the collision and now he's heading back in. What should he do – go back to his marina?'

'I'll talk to the Coastguard – I think the most likely thing is for him to go straight to the RNLI station at Harwich, that is where everything is being coordinated.'

The Coastguard confirmed that was exactly what they wanted and Saskia relayed this to Colin. Jim thought to himself that it would be a traumatic situation as Colin, the rescued woman and her possibly dead husband would all be arriving at the lifeboat station at much the same time.

A variety of different craft could be seen salvaging what little was left of the Santania and the Ocean Traveller was being manoeuvred on to its berth at Felixstowe. Two ambulances and three police cars had arrived at the RNLI station.

Some thirty minutes later the news came through that the ambulance crew had failed to revive the yachtsman and he had been confirmed dead. His distraught wife had identified him.

The radios were busy non-stop all through the rest of the morning and into the afternoon. The Seawatch afternoon watch arrived to take over at 1300 but both Jim and Saskia stayed on throughout the afternoon. The lookout was full of people and the sea was still really busy as all sorts of craft joined in to help search for anything related to the collision.

Jim looked at Saskia. 'We are going to have to write an incident report detailing everything. Exactly what we saw and when, and what action we took.'

She looked terrified. 'Do you think Colin is in trouble Jim?'

Jim shrugged. 'Well, the rule is 'If to your starboard red appear it is your duty to keep clear.'

'What the hell does that mean?'

'It means that if on your starboard side there is another vessel whose port side is nearest you then it is up to you to keep out of its way. The other vessel has the right of way.'

She looked sick. 'I'll have to talk to Colin to find out just what happened.'

It was late afternoon before Jim felt able to leave the lookout. He looked at Steve. 'Steve, I can't face doing the incident report now – my brain is absolutely frazzled. Can Sas and I come in tomorrow morning to do it, when our heads have cleared a bit and we've had a night's sleep.'

Steve thought about it. 'Ideally we should do it now but I do understand. It's been one hell of a day. Let's all meet here at 0900 in the morning and we'll do it together then. Are you both going to be at home tonight in case I need to contact you?'

They both nodded and left. As Jim drove off he could see Saskia sat in her car on the phone. He wondered if she quite understood the situation. They had both witnessed her husband seemingly cause a collision in which a man had lost his life.

Chapter 19

Everything was a blur for Jackie Norton. The dark looming bows of a monster, getting hauled into the lifeboat, people in uniforms of all sorts and identifying the dead body of her husband.

People were kind but trying to get information from her when she was in total shock. She was relieved when daughter Mary and her husband Brian arrived but couldn't understand how they had been contacted so quickly. But she had no concept of time.

She was grateful for hot mugs of sweet tea and the foil blankets the lifeboat crew wrapped around her. She started to replay in her mind what little she could remember. The puzzlement that the other yacht had nobody at the helm, the terror as the sky darkened, the shock of the cold water, the relief of the outstretched arms.

People introduced themselves as being a policeman, a policewoman, lifeboat crew, a paramedic, a coastguard, a doctor – but it was all so confusing.

Later in the day she registered being helped into Mary and Brian's car and being driven home to Shotley. There were knocks at the door, telephones kept ringing and then she was being driven to Mary's house in Ipswich. She wondered why she wasn't crying.

Jackie was no drinker but late in the day she asked for a large brandy and then another – eventually she fell asleep on Mary's sofa.

It was only when Ocean Traveller was safely berthed in Felixstowe that Captain James Kirkwood started to take stock of what had happened. He got news of the collision over the radio and his mind raced as his new command was being manoeuvred to the dockside. He was hearing frenzied radio traffic about his ship being in a collision he hadn't seen, heard or felt.

He saw the lifeboats racing out and the immediate activity as all sorts of small craft tried to provide assistance. He was grateful for the calm professionalism of the pilot – focussing only on getting his ship safely alongside.

He talked to Harwich VTS and the Coastguard over the radio and then was straight on the phone to the shipping line's head office to report what had happened. They were immediately advising caution in talking to the press – he must stress the difficulty of guiding one of the biggest ships in the world into port and the need for all small craft to stay out of the deep-water channel.

He was distressed to hear about the death of the yachtsman but relieved to hear of the rescue of his wife. He wondered if anyone had any video footage of the collision. The pilot assured him there was absolutely nothing they could have done – even if they had seen the yacht they would never have been able to slow down or change course.

Jim slept only fitfully – Sally was enquiring, understanding and sympathetic. Of course she was shocked and worried about the impact on Colin. She even felt concerned for Saskia.

They had watched the news coverage of the collision and seen the images of Jackie Norton being helped from the lifeboat. They saw the Ocean Traveller and a covered body being taken ashore from the second lifeboat.

Colin was questioned by a coastguard and the RNLI station manager when he came alongside at the lifeboat station. They needed to know if there was anyone else involved and his account of what had happened. Later he was sympathetically questioned by a policeman and policewoman.

He tried to reassure Saskia over the phone and later in the day the volunteer lifeboat escorted him back to his marina. He thanked them and sat alone on Tulip until he felt able to drive home. Saskia flung her arms around him and cried with relief.

They talked into the night and neither of them got a wink of sleep. They drank coffee and Saskia showered before returning to the lookout to meet up with Jim and Steve.

They were already there when she arrived.

Steve spoke first. 'How are you and how is your husband?'

'As well as can be expected I guess. I think he's in shock – neither of us have had any sleep.'

Jim nodded understandingly. 'I'm sorry Sas, I know you want to be with Colin but we'll get this report done ASAP and let you get back to him.'

Steve said. 'Right now the press don't seem to have got wind of many of the details. When they realise the wife of the other yachtsman involved actually witnessed what happened because she was on duty at Seawatch we can expect them to pester the life out of us. I'll try to get all enquiries channelled through me and keep them away from you and Colin as much as I can but you know what they're like.'

She nodded. 'Well the police have said they will need to talk to him today so hopefully they can help shield him a bit. We feel so awful for the wife - she must be absolutely traumatised. I hope somebody can help to keep the press away from her.'

Steve nodded. 'Okay, let's get started – the sooner we get this incident report done the sooner you can go home.'

'So, Jim tell me what you saw and what you did.'

Jim outlined the radio contact with Tulip and pointed to the timings in the log of when he had logged the details and positions of Stena Hollandica, Ocean Traveller, Tulip and Santania. He explained the two yachts had followed the Stena out of the estuary and looked to be positioning themselves to keep to port of the deep-water channel and cross it after the Ocean Traveller had passed them.

He explained how they were both carefully watching the situation – Saskia through the big powerful binoculars and him through the smaller handheld bins. He said that both he and Saskia had been puzzled that Tulip wasn't turning further to port and that at the crucial moment he couldn't see Colin at the helm.

At this point Saskia interjected. 'No, that's not right. I could see him all the time, he was just bending down for a moment. I don't

157

know why the other boat suddenly turned hard to starboard – there was no need for him to do that.'

Jim was shocked. 'No Sas, that's not right. We were both talking about how we were surprised Tulip hadn't changed course to port and we couldn't understand why we couldn't even see Colin.'

'No Jim. I'm sorry – I had the better view because I was on the big bins. I know what happened.'

Jim shook his head. 'Well let's listen to the audio tape – let's find out just what we both said at the time.'

Now it was Steve who shook his head. 'We can't do that – there's no tape in the machine.'

Jim was open mouthed. 'What? There must be, I pressed the record button before I did anything else.'

Steve looked at him enquiringly. 'Didn't you look to see that it had actually started recording?'

'No, all hell was breaking loose. I didn't want to waste a second. I just pressed the button and rang 999.'

Now Steve looked at both of them. 'And neither of you has removed a tape from the machine?'

They both shook their heads. Saskia said, 'I didn't even know we had a tape machine. This is my first real incident in Seawatch – I didn't know what the procedure was. I just took my lead from Jim.'

Steve said. 'There is always a tape in the machine, ready to be used for the next incident. I check it regularly.'

Steve's mobile rang. Jim looked at Saskia questioningly – she avoided his eyes.

Steve said. 'The police are downstairs wanting to talk to me. If you both wait here we'll continue this as soon as I can get back.'

As soon as they were alone Jim glared at Saskia. 'What the hell is going on – we both know what really happened.'

She looked at her feet. 'Look Jim, I've been up all bloody night with Colin, going over this again and again. He's in a hell of a state – he's at his wits end.'

'So what did happen? Does he accept it was his fault?'

'He got distracted at the crucial moment. He was watching the Santania, expecting it to go past him, and then his mobile rang. He went down to the cabin to get it and then dropped it before he answered it. When he got back to the wheel he was too late to change course.'

Jim breathed out. 'I wondered if it was something like that. This is a terrible situation for both of you Sas but we have to tell the truth. We can't file a dishonest incident report.'

'If this ends up in court Colin and me will be ruined. The woman on the yacht will sue Colin for every penny we've got and I tell you Jim, we would lose everything. It would ruin Colin's life - and mine. I need your help.'

'I know it's a dreadful situation Sas but think about the alternative. You can't both lie your way out of this and also expect me to perjure myself.'

'I'm sorry but I'm begging for your help Jim. If you and I just bend the truth a bit on the report. It doesn't seem that anyone has any video footage of what happened – there are only four people who know what happened. Whatever Jackie Norton says it would be her word against three of us.'

'And you think that would be fair on a woman who's just lost her husband through someone's negligence?'

'I know it's wrong Jim but please, I'm begging you. I just need you to say you couldn't see well enough through the hand-held bins. It's not really lying – I did have a better view than you.'

'Yeah and that enabled you to see that it was Colin's fault.'

Steve walked back in. 'It was just routine stuff – they are checking on details and at some stage they'll want to talk to both of you. Anyway – let's get back to the report.'

Jim's mind was in turmoil. 'We've got a problem Steve. I'm afraid Saskia and I can't agree on just what we saw. My view is that through the smaller bins I saw Tulip fail to follow the rule of the road and that effectively pushed Santania into danger. Sas' view is that she doesn't see it that way. She thinks Colin stayed at the wheel and Santania made an ill-judged turn across the bows of Ocean Traveller.'

A wide-eyed Steve blew through his teeth. 'Bloody hell – I don't believe this. I don't know if we've ever had a situation where two watchkeepers disagree over just what happened in an incident. This is an incredibly difficult situation. Especially when one of you is married to one of the parties directly involved. I've been on to the guys at Coastwatch and they couldn't see anything – their view was blocked by the new housing development near their tower. So your evidence is going to be absolutely crucial.'

Jim said. 'I can only put into writing my view of what I honestly saw and the actions I took. Anything else would be plain wrong. I joined Seawatch to try to do a little something for the community – I know that might sound pompous but I honestly thought I might even save a life one day. To deliberately falsify the log and write an incident report full of lies is something I just can't do. I've loved doing watches with you Sas and there's no way I want to drop Colin in it but this is all a step too far. I'd be a total fraud if I lied about this.'

Saskia looked angry. 'And I can only say what I saw and I had the better view because I was using the fixed binoculars which are way more powerful than what Jim was using. I'm not lying and I won't go along with a different view just to keep the peace. I don't believe my husband did make a mistake and so I'm not going to lie either'.

Steve looked from one to the other of them and shook his head. 'Bloody hell – this is a right mess and no mistake.'

Jim didn't know what to do. He held back from telling Steve that while he was talking to the police Saskia had actually admitted that both Colin and she knew that he'd made a terrible mistake. If he did it would only be his word against hers as he knew she would deny it.

161

It took the three of them all morning to do the report and none of them were happy with it. It detailed two conflicting views and from Steve's point of view it was a mess that was sure to result in more questions, an enquiry and probably a court case. He couldn't force either of them to change their opinion. It certainly didn't reflect well on Seawatch and Steve felt really mad about the whole situation.

As they left the building they both headed for their cars, but not before Saskia had one last parting shot before she drove off.

'I'm sorry Jim but we need your help and we are desperate. If you can't go along with me on this then I promise you that you'll be sorry.'

Chapter 20

Jackie Norton watched the BBC news. The aftermath of the disaster was still unfolding, with a special piece featuring the head of the Coastguard service speaking about the need for small craft to keep out of the way of the big boys. His message was that the deep-water channels were for big ships only. Small craft should be aware that a big container ship had a very limited view ahead of it and no ability to stop or change course quickly.

It made her feel that both Chris and the other yacht were being criticised but she knew it was the other yacht's fault. Maybe both of them shouldn't even have been anywhere near the deep-water channel. The looming bows of Ocean Traveller blocking out the sunlight was a recurring nightmare still, as was the panic on Chris's face when he couldn't see anyone at the helm of Tulip.

She knew she was very lucky to be alive – apart from some bruising to her legs, which was probably caused by being hauled from the water – she didn't have a scratch on her. She didn't feel lucky though – part of her wished she had been taken along with Chris. They had been so happy and were really enjoying their retirement.

Mary's husband Brian said she should sue the other yachtsman but right now she didn't even want to think about that. She didn't want to do anything other than hide away and let Mary shield her from the outside world. The thought of more interviews with police, calling a solicitor and preparing for a stressful court case filled her with dread. What was the point? If she won she would only end up with money and what use was that. It wouldn't bring Chris back and she had enough money to see her through the rest of her days – which she now hoped wouldn't be too many. No, her life was effectively over. She wanted to go to sleep and never wake up again.

Steve phoned Jim. 'Hi Jim – the police want to see both you and Saskia separately to get statements. Have you talked to her any more?'

'No, it's awkward Steve. I don't know what I can do apart from stating on the report what I believe I saw. It's not the same as what Sas saw and I guess she's right in saying that she was using the best bins, but I can't lie. I know what I saw.'

'That's right – you've got to state what you believe to be the facts. This is all a bloody mess for Seawatch though. It seems that you were the only two witnesses and it's embarrassing for Seawatch that you don't agree. There's one key question I want to ask you though Jim – what do you honestly think happened to that tape.'

'I'll tell you what I think off the record Steve. Just between you and me, I think Sas took it. I'm certain I told her we record all incidents on tape when she first joined and we were doing some training.'

'Bloody hell Jim – that's quite some allegation.'

'It's just my personal view. I wouldn't write that down and I wouldn't say that to the police or anyone else but it's what I think.'

Sally answered the phone just after Jim left for a walk along the front.

'Hi Sal, it's Sas. Can I have a word with Jim please?'

'No, he's just gone for a walk. Can I get him to call you back?'

'Yes please Sal. We've both got to give statements to the police and I wanted to just have a word with Jim first. It's all such a bloody mess. Colin's in a right state.'

'Yeah, I can imagine. Look, I'll get him to call you as soon as he gets back.'

'Okay, thanks. Oh and Sal – one other little thing. I've lost a gold earring and I wondered if I dropped it in Jim's car when he took me home from the Seawatch training session a couple of weeks back. Could you ask him to just have a look for it please?'

As soon as Jim set foot in the door he was collared by Sal.

'Saskia phoned – she wants you to call her to talk about the statements you've got to make. And, she wants you to look for her earring in your car. She thinks she might have dropped it when you took her home.'

'Oh, okay. That will be awkward – about the statements.'

'What was she doing in your car? You didn't tell me you took her home.'

'No, I didn't think. She'd walked to the training session and didn't want to walk home in the dark. She must have been in my car for all of about two minutes.'

'I'd like you to tell me everything when it comes to that woman. I don't trust her one inch.'

Jim made himself a coffee and took it, the paper and the phone down the garden. He sat and thought. What a devious bloody woman she is – and clever. This was a very obvious shot across his bows. Just letting him know she was willing to tell Sal everything if he wouldn't play ball.

He called her. 'Hi Sas – what are we going to do about these statements then?'

'I just need you to cooperate Jim. I need you to say that you've been thinking about it all and you've realised that I did indeed have the better view as I was using the big bins.'

'You want me to lie Sas – and I'm not prepared to I'm afraid. A man died and he's left a broken wife who is probably going to want to see justice done. Perjury is a very serious crime and why should I open myself up to that?'

'I'm begging you Jim. Colin is at his wits end and if this ends up in court he could be in big trouble. He could end up in prison and we could lose every bloody penny we've got. I thought you were a friend of mine. Do you want to see me end up on the street?'

'I'm sorry Sas but it will be best for everyone if we all tell the truth and Colin pleads mitigating circumstances. He could say he expected Santania to drop back so they could both have passed safely to port of Ocean Traveller. It is debatable just how the blame gets apportioned.'

'But you told me Colin didn't obey the rule of the road. This thing about 'if to starboard red appear'.

166

'Yeah, that does count against him but because Santania came from behind that does cloud the issue. He could claim that Santania broke the rules relating to overtaking vessels. The bigger problem is Colin disappearing from view – he clearly wasn't in control of Tulip at the crucial moment.'

'That's why I need you to say you've changed your mind and you couldn't see as well as I could.'

'I'm sorry Sas – I still had a good view, even through the hand-held bins. If I said I didn't that would be a blatant lie.'

'Look Jim – I need your help. I'm pleading with you. You wouldn't want Sal to know you're sleeping with me.'

'What! What the hell are you talking about? I'm not bloody sleeping with you for christ's sake.'

'You know that Jim and I know that but do you think Sally will believe you when you deny it?'

The anger surged through him. 'So it comes down to blackmail does it? I'm really seeing you in the true light now. I know you're worried but I can't believe you'd sink to this.'

'I'll do anything Jim if it keeps my husband out of prison and we can avoid financial ruin. I don't want to do this to you. All it takes is for you to say you've thought it through at great length and you've changed your mind.'

'You're prepared to lie to try and force me to lie.'

'I'm prepared to do anything – I'm sorry Jim.'

He ended the call – his head was spinning. How the hell had it come to this. A crisis of conscience if ever there was one.

Colin had barely left the apartment since the day of the collision. He had been questioned by the lifeboat station manager and the coastguard and he'd made a statement to the police but he had stopped answering the phone and was in denial.

The collision had been bad enough but then a sleepless night of talking everything through with Sas had left him totally stressed out. Admitting to her that he'd let his yacht insurance lapse had resulted in Sas going into complete meltdown. She had ranted, raged and even slapped him hard across the face and he knew he deserved it all.

Knowing that the accident was really caused by him buggering about with his phone gave him guilt feelings the like of which he'd never known before. Then the realisation that because he'd become so hopeless at sorting out routine admin he now had no cover for any claim that might be made by Jackie Norton.

He'd had perfectly good insurance but when it came to renewal time they wanted to jack the price up by what he thought was an exorbitant amount. He'd haggled over the phone, without much success, and started getting alternative quotes online. Eventually the insurance expired and he hadn't got around to sorting out a better deal.

He felt sick when he checked the paperwork and realised his cover had ceased two weeks back. It would have given him three million pounds public liability cover in the event of a collision resulting in death and now he had zilch cover. Not a single bloody penny.

Sas had starkly painted the nightmare scenario that could now unfold. He could be prosecuted for negligence and sued by Jackie Norton. With no insurance that could run into millions. He could end up in prison and bankrupt. Selling the apartment and Tulip and using all their savings would only be a drop in the ocean.

As he sank into a pit of despair Sas had outlined her plan for how he could attempt to wriggle out of the nightmare. She would convince Jim to go along with her story that Tulip hadn't forced Santania into the path of Ocean Traveller. She would say she'd had the best view of anyone and she would say that Tulip had stayed on a consistent course and that Colin was at the helm and in control throughout the incident. Chris Norton had made a terrible error of judgement and turned into the path of one of the biggest container ships in the world. Colin would have to go along with this scenario in all his dealings with the police, RNLI and Coastguard officers.

He had felt terrible about this – knowing that really it was his fault but weighed against that was the fear of financial ruin and imprisonment. Eventually and very reluctantly he'd agreed to go along with her. When he attended the local police station he made what he knew was a false statement but he had signed it anyway.

He kept thinking about Jackie Norton. She was totally blameless, had lost her husband and their yacht and could now be denied justice by their lies and deceit. He kept telling Sas how dreadful it was and how he should come clean and take the consequences. She kept telling him to think about prison, bankruptcy and homelessness.

169

He told her how ashamed he felt about stitching up Jim when he was totally blameless. In his darkest moments in the middle of the night he'd thought about downing a bottle of scotch with all the many painkillers in their bathroom cabinet. How many paracetamol and how much whisky do you have to take to be sure of ending it all? He'd probably cock that up as well and come round in Ipswich hospital in two days time having had his stomach pumped out.

He wondered about stopping the car in the middle of the Orwell bridge in the middle of the night and just leaping over the edge. Would he misjudge the tide and end up alive but with multiple injuries – stuck in the mud and being dragged out by the coastguard?

Sas told him she loved him and wanted to protect him. He agonised over what he thought were the driving forces for Sas – to what extent did she want to save him from prison and to what extent did she want to save herself from financial ruin? He wanted to believe it was only love for him that would lead her to such desperate measures. All his pride was deserting him. How low could he sink?

Chapter 21

Jackie Norton's son-in-law Brian was persistent. He kept talking about the terrible injustice of it all and how Jackie couldn't let the other yachtsman get away with it. She had no appetite for a court battle and just wanted to hide away.

'Look Brian – I know you've got my best interests at heart but we haven't even got Chris' funeral arranged yet.'

'I know – I'm sorry but I just think we should get the ball rolling. I've got a mate who's a solicitor in Ipswich and he thinks you should definitely progress this.'

'So you've already spoken to this solicitor? Without getting my agreement first.'

'Oh he's a mate Jackie – we were talking about something else and off the back of that I told him what had happened to you.'

'If I wanted to sue anyone I wouldn't even know where to start.'

'Well I did a bit of research on the net. If you have been involved in a collision at sea and you believe the other party was at fault you can take the owner of the other vessel to the Admiralty Court. I can download the admiralty claim form and help you with it. Apparently cases like this are decided by a high court judge or the Admiralty Registrar.'

'Oh my god – you have been busy. It's too soon – I've hardly taken in what happened. My head's all over the place.'

'Of course Jackie, I understand. Have a think about it and tell me when you feel ready to do something. My mate says he'd be happy to represent you on a 'no win – no fee' basis.'

'And I'd be happy if everyone backed off and left me alone.'

She was furious. What was Brian's motivation? Did he think this would boost her estate when she finally popped her clogs and left everything to Mary? Jackie reached for the gin bottle and helped herself to a large one.

Jim attended the police station, wrote what he believed to be a totally accurate statement of events and signed it. He'd been awake half the night agonising over what to do and eventually decided he had to tell the truth. If need be he'd have to tell Sal the whole sorry story and hope to hell she believed him.

He felt relief when he left the police station. He had now written an honest incident report for Seawatch and given an honest statement to the police. He'd done the right thing but was it the smart thing? If he'd just kept his mouth shut and agreed that Sas had the best view he could avoid so much hassle. But that would mean lying and doing the dirty on Jackie Norton. Now he had to figure out how best to deal with blackmail and how to hold on to his wife.

He wondered why he'd ever let himself get tangled up with Sas. Yes, she was a looker and a very sexy woman and he guessed he'd been flattered when she came on to him. But he was a 64 year old and although he guessed he'd aged reasonably well he was no Brad Pitt. Okay, he was fairly well off and he figured the house must seem impressive but why would someone like her grope him in his car after a two minute ride home from a meeting? It was bizarre. She had a good looking husband and they were comfortably well off. He understood her motive for blackmailing him but not her motive for making advances to him even before the collision happened.

Jim knew he'd been vain when she first started to show an interest in him. How many men would shun an opportunity like she'd presented him with. He had been struck right from the outset – when he first saw her sat on that stool at the yacht club bar. He'd studied her bum through the binoculars when she left the tower after that first visit with Colin. He'd used the anonymity of his sunglasses to check out her curves when she was lying by his pool. He'd been a stupid old fool – taken in by a real life femme fatal.

Press interest from the national media was easing up now but the local media were still giving the collision loads of coverage – examining it from every angle. They had obviously been pestering Steve Blake, the station manager, but he had been stonewalling, saying the matter may result in a court enquiry and so he couldn't say anything that might jeopardise that. The owners of Ocean Traveller had given a similar response, so had the local coastguard and so had both tug skippers.

The media had now resorted to generalised articles. One questioning why anyone could take a small boat out to sea without any training or qualifications. They didn't know that either of the yachtsmen involved weren't qualified but they were querying why there wasn't some equivalent to the driving test for boat owners. If you had to be qualified to drive a car why was a boat any different?

Another article queried why small craft often didn't keep well clear of large vessels. There were many instances of yachts crossing the deep-water channel in the wrong place at the wrong time. The reporter asked why action wasn't taken against the owner of any small craft doing something stupid. Occasionally they would be ticked off but why was nobody charged with the marine equivalent of dangerous driving or driving without due care and attention?

Another questioned why there wasn't some sort of CCTV system that monitored the approaches to the UK's biggest container port and automatically recorded all the movements. It was amazing that nobody had come forward with any film footage of any sort. It would have been too far out for anyone on the shore to have captured anything useful on a phone. Both of the tugs attending to Ocean Traveller would have had their view of both yachts totally obscured by the ship. Seawatch had no camera system that had a better view than either Sas or Jim had through their binoculars. No – in this age of surveillance it was surprising that nobody else had witnessed quite what happened.

If it had been a road accident somebody would probably have had dashcam footage and the police investigators would have been able to study tyre marks on the road. But the sea was quick to cover the tracks of all craft – especially when the waters were churned up by an enormous ship passing through at the time of the crash.

Both the police and the coastguard had repeatedly put out requests for anyone who had any film footage or stills that might be of any possible use to contact them. They asked if anyone just happened to be looking at the scene through binoculars but everything had drawn a complete blank. It seemed to be a fact that only two people were watching and those two people disagreed with each other.

When the media cottoned on to the fact that one of those two people was married to one of the yacht skippers involved they did everything they could to talk to either Colin or Saskia. When they stopped taking calls and answering the door the press tried to make contact with their neighbours, members of Colin's yacht club and various members of Seawatch. Luckily for Colin and Saskia nobody was prepared to dish any dirt.

 Two neighbours said they were lovely people and they couldn't believe what had happened. One yacht owner said that he knew Colin and had always found him to be a totally conscientious and responsible owner who kept his boat in lovely condition. The barman and the waitress at the yacht club both said he was a lovely guy who often ate and drank there.

The lead story in today's local paper was headlined. 'Yacht crash skipper's wife was watching'. It detailed the fact that the wife of the other yacht involved in the collision was a member of Seawatch and was on duty at the time of the incident. The article was accompanied by pictures of the Seawatch lookout and of Ocean Traveller. Similar but smaller stories appeared on the inside pages of most national dailies.

The local radio stations were also headlining the same story and making repeated calls for 'anyone who may have witnessed the incident or has any film footage or pictures that could be of assistance to the investigation are asked to contact Felixstowe police station'. They carried two interviews with local yacht skippers which really added nothing to the story other than to reinforce the message about staying well away from large vessels. One crackpot member of the public even called the radio station to question whether pleasure craft should be allowed to use the estuary at all when there were such large ships in the area.

Chapter 22

Jim was sat at the computer in his study doing his usual daily browsing on the net. He searched for and read all the stories relating to the collision. He browsed the local paper, the Telegraph, The Guardian and both BBC and MSN news.

He looked at stock markets across the world, business news, FX rates and the price of Brent Crude. All things he did every day to keep track of what was happening in the world economy – a throwback to his days as an accountant.

He browsed the sports news to see what was happening in football, F1, golf and cricket and he checked out the weather forecast.

He turned to email and looked at the contents of his in-box. There was the usual junk mail, a couple of routine Seawatch notices, a stock market briefing sheet, two requests to complete surveys relating to stuff he'd bought from Amazon and then one more.

The subject heading was 'Information Required' and it was from an anonymous gmail.co.uk address of 'taxinv39716'. It read as follows:

'Dear Mr. Ellis

I represent a unit working on behalf of HMRC and am currently engaged in an investigation into tax receipts related to trading in stocks and shares.

This investigation goes back to the tax year 2001/02 and I would be grateful if you would reply to this email giving a summary of any transactions relating to the trading of any individual blocks of shares by you, since the 2001/02 tax year, which exceed the sum of £10,000.

The information we hold in your file shows that your occupation is 'Retired Chartered Accountant'. Your address is Savannah, Golf Road, Felixstowe, IP11 7NG. The landline telephone number is 01394-982364 and the mobile number is 07941-078992. Please let me know if any of this is incorrect.

We may contact you by letter or telephone call but at this stage I am unable to communicate with you via any means other than email.

I assure you all communication will be in total confidence.

I would be grateful if you could reply by email as soon as possible.

Regards

John Chambers'

Jim's heart was racing with blind panic. His first reaction to any scary or dubious emails was to take his time and act rationally. How genuine was it? The email address almost made it appear that it was a tax invoice - one of those spam emails that purported to relate to a genuine business transaction but was actually some sad con artist sitting in his bedroom trying to get you to hand over your bank details.

It didn't have the usual grammatical errors and dubious phraseology of the typical Nigerian scammer. He wondered if he should check with HMRC to see whether they thought it was dodgy, but even if it was he didn't want to be alerting HMRC to anything anyway.

He googled 'taxinv' and the full email address but nothing showed up. He tried searching for all derivations of 'Tax Investigations' but amongst the many results there was nothing that helped in any way.

He mused that the good thing was that he had never personally actually bought or sold any shares relating to Data Finance. The deal hadn't worked that way – he had been paid a consultancy fee that officially related to general advice on a range of different businesses. Yes, shares had been traded but not in his name. All his dealings had been with his old friend Roy Manning – for services rendered to Data Finance. There was nothing relating directly to Jim's client that was taken over.

He made himself take a few deep breaths and looked out to sea, trying to compose himself. How the hell had this suddenly happened after all these years? Was it in some way related to the fact that he was now central to a major news story?

He thought he was pretty savvy at sussing out dodgy emails but he had nearly been caught out only last week. He was expecting Fed-Ex to deliver a new shredding machine and on the due day there was an email in his inbox headed 'Sorry you were out when we tried to deliver today.' There was a link to click on to arrange re-delivery and he was just about to when a sixth sense told him to check first. He googled 'Fed-Ex scam emails about delivery' and sure enough found that it was dodgy and that clicking on the link exposed your computer to a virus. The shredder duly arrived later in the day.

He googled 'John Chambers' and there were millions of matches and so he looked on Facebook, only to find well over 200 John Chambers. It was obviously a common name and it would take a lot of work to examine the Facebook pages of over 200 people and the chances were this particular John Chambers wasn't on there anyway.

He re-read the email over and over again. The email was obviously letting him know the sender had a certain amount of information about him. The one thing it didn't contain was his tax reference and he thought that would have been included to convince him of its authenticity.

Eventually he composed his reply:

'Dear Mr. Chambers.

I received your email and before replying with any details of my financial affairs I would just like to double check that you are who you say you are.

If you are working on behalf of HMRC you will know my Tax Reference (National Insurance number) and my UTR number. If you can please send me another email stating these details I will then be happy to provide the information you require.

Regards

James Ellis'

The more Jim thought about it the more he convinced himself the email wasn't genuine. It was one thing for somebody to know his occupation, address and phone numbers but only HMRC would have the reference numbers. He started to breathe normally again. It still begged the question of what the hell was going on and why now?

It was later the same day when he got a reply from the mysterious John Chambers.

'Dear Mr. Ellis

Thank you for your reply. I quite understand you wanting to check the authenticity of my earlier email and it is only right and proper that you should do so.

On your file we have a National Insurance number of YL 47 53 64 B and a Unique Taxpayer Reference of 39391366804.

I look forward to you supplying the requested details at your earliest convenience.

Regards

John Chambers

Jim grabbed his tax file from the filing cabinet and checked. 'Oh shit'.

The hairs stood up on the back of his neck. What the hell was going on? Was it just coincidence that HMRC were investigating him now or had they seen his name in the news? He would have liked to talk all this through with Sal – get someone else's view on what was going on. He felt his brain was all over the place. He hadn't been sleeping properly with all the worries surrounding the collision and now to get this on top of everything else was sending him into meltdown.

He couldn't talk it through with Sal because she had never known anything about his dodgy dealing. What with her having to deal with the stress of his involvement with the collision, and the anger she harboured about Saskia, now wasn't the time to load something else on her. Especially something that he had kept to himself and that sounded really suspicious. He wished he'd told her a long time ago – before the wedding. She deserved to know where all his wealth had come from. She had a touching faith that Jim had made it all from running a successful business and using his knowledge and experience to invest wisely.

She knew nothing of business and finance but he felt she was scrupulously honest and would take a very different view of her husband if she only knew the facts.

Eventually he composed another email.

'Dear Mr. Chambers

Thank you for supplying the details I requested. I am happy to provide any information you require but I can assure you I didn't have any share transactions in excess of £10,000 in the period from the 2001/02 tax year right through to the present day.

I have personally traded shares on a number of occasions but always in smaller transactions. I have received many dividend payments over the years and have always declared these on my annual tax returns and paid any due tax accordingly.

As a chartered accountant I have always kept scrupulous records and can provide more specific details of individual share trading transactions if required.

Regards

James Ellis'

He gazed out to sea and reflected. He was telling the truth. It wasn't the share trading that was dubious, it had been his use of inside knowledge and the breach of a client confidentiality agreement that was dodgy.

The business accounts would show payments from Data Finance but did John Chambers even know who Data Finance were? If he did, was he examining share trading that had been carried out by Roy Manning, using inside knowledge provided by Jim?

He felt so tense his stomach was aching. Was he getting a recurrence of his old ulcer trouble? He went to the bathroom cabinet and took a Nexium tablet with a glass of water.

Chapter 23

Saskia looked at her computer screen and smiled. She definitely had him rattled now.

With most of a lifetime in IT it had been easy to create a fake email address and become John Chambers. Jim's request for his tax refence numbers had required a call to Phil Jenkinson though. Phil was an old work colleague and one-time boyfriend she had kept in touch with over the years.

He now worked as a programmer with HMRC and owed Sas a favour anyway relating to a dodgy job reference she had once provided for him. It had only needed a phone call and within the hour Phil had supplied the details she needed.

Jim would be really squirming now. She smiled to herself – don't get pissed and own up to naughty stuff if you don't want it to come back and bite you in the bum.

He was out for a walk when she called his landline but Sally answered.

'Hi Sal. It's Sas – I'm sorry but I need to speak to Jim again – something else has come up about the collision.'

'He's gone to the shops – I'll have to get him to call you back.'

'Okay Sal, thanks. By the way, do you know if he had any luck finding my earring?'

'I duuno – you'll have to ask him. I didn't even know you'd been in his car. I don't know what you two get up to.'

'Oh, lighten up Sal. It's only an earring. It could have been worse – it could have been my knickers.'

She laughed, but Sally didn't. She slammed the phone down.

Saskia decided she would have to start moving things on more quickly. Jim needed to see sense and own up to having been wrong about what he'd seen. She wondered what he'd told Sally about what happened and about their difference of opinion. She also wondered what he might have told anyone else.

The phone rang. 'Hi Sas, it's Jim. Sal said you were trying to get me.'

'Yeah, I need to know what's happening Jim. Have you had a change of mind?'

'No, I haven't Sas. I've made my statement at the police station and it's essentially the same as what I put in the incident report. It's honest – I've written down what I know I saw. I can't change it – that would just make me look stupid now and it would be a terrible thing to do to Jackie Norton.'

'Well, that's just dumb. You need to get your brain together to help Colin and you need to help me.'

'How can I Sas? You want me to lie and lying in court is perjury. That's a bloody serious offence – I'm not ending up in a cell for you.'

'I want your help Jim. I've been in touch with an old friend of mine. His name is John Chambers – have you heard from him?'

He gasped audibly and there was a long pause. 'Jesus, I don't believe this is happening. You won't stop at anything will you?'

'I've told you – we're desperate.'

'How do you know John Chambers?'

'Oh, he's an old mate. He was my boyfriend for several years – we lived together in London and we've always kept in touch.'

'And he's prepared to investigate me just because you tell him to?'

'It doesn't have to be like this Jim. He could initiate a full investigation into you and your old company or he could be persuaded to back off and leave you alone. It's your choice.'

'Amazing, absolutely bloody amazing. Are you a witch?'

'I'm just a woman who doesn't want to see her husband go to prison when it's not necessary. If you go along with me any court case or enquiry would have to return an open verdict. It would be our word against Jackie Norton's.'

'You don't have much regard for her do you? An innocent woman who's just lost her husband.'

'Well, we can't bring him back from the dead can we?'

'I'm gonna have to think about this. You've got me over a barrel – you nasty scheming bitch.'

'Oh temper, temper Jim. You need to think fast or I'll have to talk to both John and Sal. It's your choice. Time is running out.'

She ended the call. He leaned back in his chair and stared unseeingly out of his study window. Usually a single Nexium tablet fixed his stomach ache in no time – but not today.

He mused that Saskia was indeed a very dangerous woman – a witch – a she-devil. She was putting his marriage and his security at enormous risk. If he told all to Sally would she believe him? Saskia had managed to turn a few brief moments when they were alone together into something enormous. The stupid kiss when he gave her a lift home and then again when they shared a cab. She had very cleverly managed to sow seeds of doubt in Sal's mind and if she was now going to tell her they had slept together would that just seem to confirm the suspicion she'd already put into Sal's head? He knew he'd been totally stitched up by a conniving cow.

Then there was the John Chambers angle. If he dug deep enough into his background going back over the last twenty years he might just be able to find unusually large payments which would be difficult to explain away. Need he worry though? He had paid the tax. The problem was the breach of a confidentiality agreement. But would HMRC care about that? Might John Chambers refer it on to the police? Could he trigger an investigation by the fraud squad? What a bloody nightmare.

Three months ago he had never met Saskia. He was happily sailing along – enjoying life with Sal, his golf, the big house and pool, nice holidays, meals out. Everything had been just cool. And then this awful bloody woman came along. She'd seemed such a nice person when he did those first watches with her. Good looking, sexy, smart, nice personality. How wrong can you be?

Jim tried to clear his head. He had two big problems – the possibility of losing Sal and the possibility of getting found out about his dodgy dealing. He didn't want to be owning up to Sal about both things at the same time. It would be hard enough to convince her that he was being completely stitched up by Saskia and wasn't guilty of cheating on her. It would be doubly difficult if in the next breath he was telling her that a big chunk of his wealth had come about by cheating on a client.

He came to a decision. He'd never been sure about just how illicit his dealings with Data Finance and Davis & Kershaw were. He had always tended towards thinking he'd done something illegal rather than just unethical. So why didn't he go straight to the client that he'd let down all those years ago and come clean? Get the client's view on whether he felt he'd been cheated or not.

He dug out Peter Kershaw's number. Davis & Kershaw had been a client for many years before Jim ever spoke to Roy Manning about them. They had been a small software business but had sunk all their spare cash into developing the ground-breaking new system that Jim knew could elevate them to dizzy heights of success.

'Hi Peter – it's Jim Ellis here. Long time – no hear.'

'Bloody hell Jim. Thought you'd emigrated to a desert island somewhere. Lovely to hear from you. What are you doing these days?'

'Oh, I'm retired now. Married and living in Felixstowe. A lot has happened.'

They chewed the fat and spent ten minutes quizzing each other about the past. Eventually Peter said 'So what made you suddenly get in touch – didn't I pay your last invoice?'

Jim laughed. 'You always paid. One of my best customers, ever.'

So he outlined everything. How he knew Roy Manning. How he saw the opportunity for Data Finance. How he breached the confidentiality agreement between them. How all that triggered Roy to make them an offer and how when all the deals were done he received a big thank-you from Roy's company. Basically – how he got rich and ended up living in luxury.

To his amazement Peter laughed. 'So what the hell are you worried about? Good luck to you.'

'No, you don't understand Pete. I signed a confidentiality agreement with you that precluded me from passing any information about Davis & Kershaw or your products or plans on to anyone else. And I broke that agreement.'

'Well I'm glad you did. You did us a big favour. If it hadn't been for Data Finance coming in, the product would never have got to market. We had a real cash flow problem at the time – we'd sunk everything into it and we were fast running out of money. You wouldn't have known how bad it was because it was probably about nine months since you'd done our last year-end accounts.'

'Data Finance saved our bacon Jim. I know they've done really well out of it – probably better than us, but it was a win-win situation. If you did really well too then I couldn't be more pleased. That deal has seen me and my kids alright for the rest of our lives – probably the grandkids too. No, for you to be in

189

trouble I'd have to sue you and there's no way on earth I'm going to do that'.

'Wow Pete. That is such a bloody relief. Its niggled me for years. But I've still done something I shouldn't have. Ethically it's not right.'

'Ethics? Bollocks! What's gonna happen – will you get drummed out of the Institute of Chartered Accountants? Do you give a stuff if you do? No, you're worrying about nothing Jim. Enjoy your retirement.'

'Thanks Pete. I'd love to buy you a drink – in fact I'd like to buy you several. Let's meet up. I'll spend some of my ill-gotten gains on a slap-up lunch'.

'Love to Jim. Look forward to it. Take care and for god's sake stop worrying.'

He pushed the chair back, looked out to sea and breathed one huge sigh of relief. He mentally gave the finger to both Saskia and John Chambers. One nightmare sorted – one to go.

Chapter 24

Jim waited until dinner was over, the dishwasher loaded and the worktops cleaned. Sally sat on the big sofa in the lounge, put on her reading glasses and picked up the paper. Jim sat in his favourite armchair holding a glass of wine – the remains of the bottle of Rioja they had with dinner.

'Sal I've got something to tell you – something we need to talk about.'

She pushed her glasses to the end of her nose and peered over the top of them. 'Sounds serious.'

'It is. I'm being blackmailed.'

She took her glasses off and stared at him. 'What? Are you serious?'

He nodded. 'I am, it's a bloody mad situation. It's all to do with the collision.'

'Is this about Saskia?'

'Yeah – it's all about her and my refusal to go along with her and falsify my statements about what happened.'

'I knew there was something going on with all those phone calls.'

'Yeah, well basically I think the collision was all down to Colin. He got his boat into the wrong position, left the wheel to go down into the cabin just at the crucial moment and effectively forced the other yacht into the path of the container ship.'

'Yeah, well I figured that from what you've been telling me and I know that you and her haven't agreed over what you've had to put into writing – the incident report and stuff.'

'Sas is lying to try to save Colin from prosecution. All this is likely to end up in court and she wants me to pretend I didn't get a good view of what actually happened. She is saying that she was using the better binoculars – which is true, she was on the big fixed bins and they have 45 times magnification. I was using the ordinary hand held bins which only have 7 times. But they were enough – the collision was only a mile from the tower and I had a clear view. Not as good as hers but good enough for me to be certain that I know what really happened.'

'If this goes to court we will both be witnesses and Seawatch has a big problem if I give my version and she gives a completely different version. Steve is mad as hell that it makes Seawatch look really stupid and disingenuous – and it does. But – if we were to both tell the truth then it's likely that Colin will be found guilty of causing death by negligence.'

'Bloody hell – and where does blackmail come into all this?'

'Saskia is planning to make up a story about me and her sleeping together. She's threatening to tell you that and I promise you it's all a total pack of lies.'

She dropped the newspaper on the floor and blew noisily through her teeth. 'That bloody woman – I knew she was trouble. So is there any truth in this?'

'None at all. She has been coming on to me but I haven't done anything wrong. I promise you.'

'You do fancy her – I've seen the way you look at her. You can't take your eyes off her legs.'

'Oh Sal – she is a good looking woman but you know me – I clock the legs of anything in a short skirt. That's just being a typical bloke.'

'What was this business of you giving her a lift and her losing an earring in your car?'

'Oh that was nothing. She asked for a lift home from the library after that training meeting. It was dark and how could I refuse? I'd have given anyone a lift home who might have asked.'

'Have you ever kissed her?'

He knew he looked defensive. 'No, but she has kissed me. When she got out of the car that night she said thanks and just pecked me on the cheek. It was nothing.'

'Is there anything else you want to tell me?'

Jim knew he wasn't making a good job of this. 'Yes, I told her something in confidence about my financial affairs and she's been threatening to shop me to HMRC.'

Sally's eyes opened wide. 'What?'

'It's something and nothing. Umpteen years back I had a client who was developing some new software and I told a friend of mine. The upshot was my friend ended up taking a controlling stake in this company and he paid me for my advice.'

'He paid you a lot of money?'

'Yeah, about a million.'

'Bloody hell. And you shouldn't have done it?'

'No, strictly speaking I shouldn't because I'd signed a confidentiality agreement with my client. But it's not a problem – I've been in touch with the client and he's totally okay with what I did. In fact he said it did him an enormous favour. He made a ton of money out of the deal and so did my mate.'

'And so did you?'

'Yeah, I did but I declared all my earnings correctly and paid the tax due. I've always been a bit worried about breaching confidentiality but the client says good luck to me – he's glad I did and there's no problem. It would be a problem if the client thought I'd stitched him up but that's not the case – he got rich out of it.'

'So how does Saskia know all about this? I'm your wife and you've never told me a word of this.'

'Well it goes back to that Seawatch dinner – the night you were busy with your play. I had a load to drink as you know – G&Ts, wine and then at the end a couple of brandies. Saskia came over to speak to me and she'd been drinking as well. She was talking about what a goody-goody I was and I said I hadn't always been squeaky clean.'

'So you unloaded all this on to that nasty devious cow. I don't believe I'm really hearing this. So what happened next?'

Jim shifted his feet uncomfortably. 'She asked if we could share a cab home and I couldn't say no.'

'Go on.'

'Well it was a two minute journey to hers and as she got out she said goodnight and kissed me.'

'Kissed you how?

'On the lips. I was totally gobsmacked. I couldn't believe she did it – and she sort of grabbed me as she got out of the car.'

'Sort of grabbed you how, where?'

'Between the legs.'

'And did you like it?'

'Oh, come on Sal. I honestly couldn't believe what she'd done but I figured we were both pissed and it was a mad moment. Something she'd never ever have done if she was sober.'

'And so now she's got two things on you. Quite apart from snogging my husband and groping him she knows you were involved in some dodgy dealing.'

'Oh Sal, you make it sound a hundred times worse than it was.'

'Well it doesn't sound great does it. I don't know if I'm madder about that slut snogging my husband or about my husband deciding he will divulge a secret about dodgy money he's made to her, when he's never ever thought to tell me about it.'

'Strictly speaking I've never kissed her and I certainly haven't snogged her. The first time she kissed me on the cheek and the second time she kissed me on the mouth. Both times as she was getting out of a car – I had no time to react, to do anything or say anything. As for the money I'd never have told anyone if I hadn't got completely off my head on booze.'

'Well I've seen you smashed a few times and you've never decided to tell me any dodgy secrets. What the hell were you thinking of?'

'I wasn't thinking anything Sal – I was just hammered.'

'Does Colin know what she's doing? That his wife snogged a man she's now blackmailing? Does he know about the financial stuff?'

'I think he knows everything and Saskia has told him that he's got to go along with it all if he wants to stay out of prison. I bet he doesn't want to go along with it but she wears the trousers in that marriage. He's a decent guy – probably wants to just hold his hands up and admit to it all.'

'So she's controlling both of you.'

'I'm not letting her control me Sal. I'm going to tell her to do her worst. I told the truth in the Seawatch incident report and I told the truth in my statement to the police and now I'm telling the truth to my wife. I need you to believe me and then she'll have no hold over me. I know in my own mind that I've done nothing wrong so please believe me.'

She started to cry and when he tried to put his arm around her she shrugged it off. 'I don't know what to believe. I'm going to bed – on my own.'

Jim just sat there for a while – head in hands. He had a very large brandy and took himself off to the spare bedroom at the far end of the house. Eventually he dozed off into a fitful troubled sleep.

He stumbled out of bed just after seven and went down to the kitchen to make coffee. He thought he would take Sal's into the main bedroom, but she wasn't there. He looked out of the front windows – her car was gone.

Chapter 25

Saskia was mad with Colin. He seemed to have given up. He moped around the apartment all day in total silence.

'If we're going to get out of this mess you need to buck your bloody ideas up. Don't just leave everything to me.'

'What can I do Sas? I've buggered everything up. I am just so sorry but I don't know what to do.'

'Well if Jim doesn't buckle I don't know what to do either.'

'It's not right Sas – what you're doing to him.'

'He's just being pig-headed. He's so bloody self-righteous. Right from the beginning he could just have said he didn't really see what happened. He didn't need to lie – he could just have kept quiet. All that would have gone down in the incident report was what I said I had seen.'

'But he knows that would have been wrong. I know you were just trying to protect me but let's face it he was being honest and you weren't.'

'So you're just gonna give up are you? Plead guilty and end up in clink and leave me to sort out our bankruptcy and try to find somewhere to live. That's a great prospect.'

'You won't be homeless Sas. You've got a good pension. You'll be able to rent somewhere.'

'Oh great. Some little flea infested flat. I don't know why I ever agreed to have this place in your name.'

'You know why we agreed to it Sas. It was only for tax reasons. It made sense at the time.'

'Well it doesn't make any bloody sense now. And I put my money into your sodding boat. That was a great investment. That brought us loads of joy didn't it?'

'I don't know what to say Sas. It's all my fault and I am just so sorry. I bet you wish you'd never met me.'

'Yeah, right now that is exactly how I feel. But I'm the realist – I know we've got to sort this and Jim is the key to me getting it fixed.'

'I dunno Sas. He might just dig his heels in.'

Steve Blake took a phone call from Andy Burton – the National Manager for Seawatch.

'Hi Steve. I've been looking at this incident report. What a bloody mess – two watchkeepers who've both seen one of our biggest incidents ever and they can't agree on what they saw. It's made us a complete bloody laughing stock.'

'I know Andy but it's all such a complicated business with one of the watchkeepers being the wife of the yachtsman who might just have caused all this.'

'Off the record Steve what do you think?'

'I honestly don't know. One half of me thinks Saskia Beaumont is lying to cover for her husband and the other half of me acknowledges she was using vastly superior bins to Jim's.'

'The report says the collision was just a fraction over one mile away from your lookout and the vis was good. When you look at a craft in that area from your lookout how well can you see it using the different bins?'

'Well through the ordinary bins I could see it pretty clearly – I'd know what type of yacht it was, the sail number if it had one and I'd be able to count how many people were visible on board. Through the big bins I'd have a far better view and I'd be able to see much more detail – I'd be able to figure out if anyone visible was wearing a lifejacket and I could read a name on the side of a boat even if the lettering was quite small.'

'So there's no doubt she had the better view but she also had the motive to lie about it.'

'Yeah, she did and Jim Ellis had no motive. You'd assume he was just telling the truth and stating what he'd seen.'

'Has Mrs. Norton started any legal proceedings do you know?'

'Not that I know Andy but I'd be surprised if she didn't. She's probably still shell shocked by it all but I think that when she gets her brain around it she'll take legal advice. Both Jim and Saskia have made statements to the police and they've been questioned by the Coastguard and RNLI. If a court decided it was negligence Jackie Norton would stand to win a fortune.'

'And the national press would be reporting how the only two witnesses were both members of Seawatch and they can't agree on what they saw. Our credibility will be shot to bloody bits.'

In fact at that very moment Jackie Norton was sitting in a solicitor's office in Ipswich. Her son-in-law Brian had been looking at the relative merits of Jackie suing Colin Beaumont directly and going through a no win – no fee solicitor.

Jackie thought it was premature that they were doing this even before Chris' funeral had taken place but Brian kept saying that they needed to just get the ball rolling at this stage. Daughter Mary had been wonderful in taking the weight off her shoulders. Without her Jackie doubted that she would have been able to deal with death certificates, undertakers and all the many admin tasks which needed sorting out.

Personally she wondered why she would go through all this just for money. She was comfortably off with generous pensions and no debts. More than anything else she wanted to have space to grieve and she wanted to avoid stress.

The solicitor's name was Charles Walker and he was an old school friend of Brian's. He assured Jackie he was at least ninety percent certain she could win this case and that the pay-out would be huge. He said he would shoulder all the risks and do all the work and she would still receive 75% of the award.

Brian had previously told her that if she sued directly she would have to pay an up-front court fee of £10,000 to start the case and solicitor's fees but that he was sure she would end up with vastly more money at the end of it all. Jackie was nervous that if she didn't win she could be left with an enormous bill and maybe paying everyone's costs.

In the end she put her foot down and took the cautious approach. The solicitor told her it would have to go through the Admiralty Court and he helped her complete something called an 'in personam' claim form. They jointly drafted a 'statement of case' which he would send to Colin Beaumont with all the other paperwork. He said Mr. Beaumont would then have to respond within 14 days of receiving this.

Apparently the judge would identify the issues in the case, work out how long the trial would last and set a date for the trial. There would probably be a pre-trial review meeting in the two months before the trial to check that everything was in place and then a wait of a few months depending on the Commercial Court lead times.

Jackie was nervous. 'I'm not sure about all this. It sounds like it will all go on for ages and I'm terrified about standing up in court.'

Walker reassured her. 'The judge will be very understanding Mrs. Norton. He knows you lost your husband in the most terrible circumstances and he will take account of the personal trauma you went through during the collision and the rescue. I will call expert witnesses, present expert reports and question the witnesses.'

'But I'll still have to speak?'

'Yes, I'm afraid so. Without your participation there can be no trial but I promise you everyone will make it as painless as possible.'

'But Colin Beaumont's lawyer will be able to grill me in front of everyone?'

'Yes, he will almost certainly want to ask questions but if you simply stick to the facts as you've told them to me then you won't have a problem, I promise you.'

'And there are no hidden costs? No win – no fee really does mean that – I don't have to pay anything, no matter what happens?'

'That's right Mrs. Norton. I take all the risk.'

'Okay then – I'm nervous as hell about all this but let's go for it.'

Chapter 26

Jim repeatedly called Sally's mobile, only to get the automated reply asking him to leave a message. He left repeated messages, each one getting progressively more desperate.

Finally, early in the afternoon, she answered.

'Oh Sal, I've been worried sick. Where are you?'

'I'm at Mum and Dad's – I needed some space.'

'Bloody hell, you're in Guildford? Did you take any clothes?'

'Yeah, I couldn't sleep and I ended up throwing a few bits in an overnight bag. I'm okay.'

'Oh Sal – I'm so so sorry. This is a sodding nightmare and it's all that cow's fault. I give you my word there's nothing going on. I've been completely and totally stitched up.'

'It's not just that woman. It's the money stuff too. I've always thought that I was so lucky to meet you and I suppose I've always been impressed by the money. Now it's a real blow to my confidence in you. What else might there be that you haven't told me?'

'There's nothing else Sal. I've been dumb getting suckered in by Saskia but I haven't done anything wrong there and that's the god honest truth of it. I have always thought that I did do something wrong financially but having talked to Peter Kershaw the other day I now find out I've been worrying for nothing for the last umpteen years. But really that's where I did wrong – I've been lucky that it all worked out really well for him and now he thanks me for it but it was still wrong. I know I breached an agreement and did something unethical.'

'I so want you to be telling me the truth Jim but I want a few days to get my head around all this. This has really shaken my confidence. I just can't tell you how much I despise that bloody woman and I'm mad that you fancied her. What the hell were you doing letting her stick her hand in your crotch?'

'I didn't let her Sal. She just grabbed me when she got out of the car. I had no time to react – or to say anything.'

'Well now you've got time to think about it. She'll probably pay you a visit if she knows I'm down here. Anyway, I'll call you tomorrow – or the next day.'

She terminated the call and when he redialled her phone was off.

Colin had a sick feeling when he saw the letter on the mat. It looked formal and ominous and it was.

Charles Walker had enclosed all the official paperwork with a covering letter of explanation. He had fourteen days to respond. He'd known this was coming. He hoped against hope that Jackie Norton might decide she couldn't face the hassle of a court case but the outcome was a no brainer. If he'd gently run in the back of another car he'd almost certainly get taken to the cleaners for it in today's world of litigation and scams.

To think he could force a yacht into the path of a container ship, which sliced it in half and killed the owner and then get away with it was just mad. He certainly didn't blame Jackie Norton for wanting to see him in court.

He reread the letter over and over again and stared uncomprehendingly at the very official looking forms. He was still sat there looking at it when Saskia came in an hour later.

She took one look at him and she knew what it was. She took the paperwork from him, scanned it and said, 'We need a solicitor.'

He couldn't think of a single word to say to her. He sat staring at the floor as she opened her tablet and googled.

Jackie Norton wanted her husband's funeral to be a quiet family affair but the press had other ideas. It was at the local church with food and drink at the yacht club afterwards.

She had expected no more than fifty people but the little church was packed. The family amounted to a total of just ten of them and then there were friends and neighbours, people she recognised from the yacht club and a whole bunch of people she didn't know at all.

Chris had always joked that when the time came he wanted people to have a good drink and a laugh at his funeral and he certainly didn't want anyone dressed in black. But as Jackie looked around she felt angry at those who seemed to have made no special attempt to dress appropriately for a funeral. There was a woman from the yacht club in a short flowery dress, a girl in three quarter length pink trousers and one man in jeans – they didn't even look like clean jeans.

The reporters didn't even make an effort to be circumspect – with some of them holding their phones and a couple even taking notes during Mary's tearful eulogy to her dad. Jackie felt dead inside and it all became a bit of a blur.

Somehow she picked herself up for the wake and went around making small talk. Nobody was insensitive enough to even mention the collision or her rescue. There were the offers of help from all and sundry – all people who knew they couldn't really help at all but felt they had to offer.

At the end Mary and Brian drove her back to their house in Ipswich. Brian fixed her a large gin and tonic and they all sat in the lounge discussing who'd been there and who hadn't.

When they'd exhausted all the small talk Jackie said, 'I'm going back home tomorrow.'

Mary looked shocked. 'Oh no Mum, it's far too soon. Stay here a few more days at least.'

'No, you've been very good but I need to start facing up to things on my own. To be honest I want some space too. I want time on my own to try to start getting my head around all this.'

'What if I come with you for the first couple of days Mum? Help you get settled in. Do some shopping for you.'

'No, it's kind of you to offer but my mind's made up.'

Mary drove her home the following day – stopping on the way at the local shop in Shotley, to pick up bread, milk and a few other essentials. The house looked so empty and quiet - Jackie mused – that's how life is going to be now – empty and quiet.

When Mary left she drove just a short way and then had to pull in to a lay-by. She sat overlooking the river and sobbed her heart out. She felt like she'd lost her dad and half of her mum.

Chapter 27

Jim tried Sally's mobile again but once again it went unanswered.

He rang Saskia. 'It's Jim, can you talk?'

'Yeah sure – have you got some good news for me?'

'Are you on your own?'

'Yeah – Colin has gone to the boat. I'm about to get dressed. I'm completely starkers at the moment – you could pop round if you like and I won't get dressed until you get here. You could choose my undies. I bet you're a stockings and suspenders fan.'

'You really are something else. That definitely wouldn't be a good idea. Look Sas, I'm phoning to tell you that you've got nothing over me any more.'

'What do you mean?'

'I came clean to Sal. I told her exactly what you were threatening me with – that you were going to tell her we'd slept together in an attempt to get me to lie about the collision.'

'And did she believe your side of it?'

'She doesn't know. We had a bad night and she took herself off to her Mum and Dad's in Surrey. That's where she is now and she's not answering my phone calls. All thanks to you.'

'And what about your dodgy dealing – I bet you didn't tell her about that.'

'I did actually and now that's been fixed. I'm in the clear.'

'How come?'

'I contacted the guy who owns the company that was my client – the one where I'd signed a confidentiality agreement, which I breached. He is totally okay with it. In fact he's more than okay – he says I did him a huge favour as the company did really well out of the takeover. He said if I hadn't done what I did they could have gone bust through cash flow problems. He hoped I'd made a ton of money out of it because he did.'

'Well, you're a lucky boy aren't you?'

'No, not if I lose my wife.'

'She'll come round Jim – she knows which side her bread is buttered on. You'll be okay but poor old Colin won't. He goes to his boat every day now – just sits there and mopes. Doesn't take her out and says he's too ashamed to even show his face in the clubhouse. You've ruined him Jim – you could have saved him but you just had to be so bloody squeaky clean.'

'Well I haven't lied and now I don't have any dark secrets to hide so you've got no hold over me any more. I hope I never see you again and I definitely won't be doing any more watches with you, no matter what happens.'

'No, you won't – I'm resigning from Seawatch. They haven't done me any favours at all. We could have had something going between us Jim. I'd have loved getting in that big bed of yours but now you've completely buggered everything up.'

Steve Blake looked at the email from Saskia Beaumont on his screen. It read:

Dear Steve

I'm sorry to have to tender my resignation from Seawatch with immediate effect.

The tragic incident has now resulted in Mrs. Norton taking my husband Colin to court and so it would be totally inappropriate for me to have any further connection with Seawatch.

I have been desperately disappointed in Jim Ellis' stance over this. His refusal to acknowledge that I had a better view of the collision than him has put my husband in a perilous position. His freedom and our future security has been put at grave risk.

I also believe that Seawatch as an organisation should have done more to support one of its watchkeepers. In our hour of need you have deserted us and I can only hope that you feel honour bound to give my husband some support when the case comes to court.

Saskia Beaumont

Steve sighed and picked up the phone to relay the news to Andy Burton.

'Steve you know you'll have to be so bloody careful what you say if you get called as a witness.'

'Well I wasn't a witness, strictly speaking.'

'No, but you are the station manager and you talked to both of them about how to complete the incident report. If you end up in a court-room you'll have to just state facts. Don't get drawn into giving any opinion by some smart-arsed lawyer.'

'No I definitely won't. All I can do is repeat what each of them told me. They were the only two people in the lookout at the time and as it turns out the only witnesses.'

'You might get cross examined about detail Steve. The capabilities of the different bins they were using – stuff like that.'

'Yeah, I know. I'll give the technical specs of the bins but I won't be drawn into what I think each of them would have been likely to see.'

'Okay Steve – just be bloody careful. Seawatch's reputation has suffered enough through this. We don't want any cock-ups that make things even worse. Keep calm and be professional.'

'Do you think I'm not usually then Andy?'

'I'm sorry Steve – I didn't phrase that very well. You've always been a first-class Station Manager and I have total confidence in you. I just don't want some clever clogs lawyer making a mug out of you. You don't deserve that and neither does Seawatch.'

'I'll be careful Andy. Bloody amazing though isn't it? We're all volunteers just trying to do something public spirited and we end up in a fiasco like this. It's gonna make a lot of our volunteers wonder if they need this sort of hassle.'

Jim was having a dismal weekend. Sally's phone was off and she'd said he wasn't to call her parent's landline number. The weather was dull and his mood was worse.

He wandered aimlessly around the house. Torturing himself by looking at all the signs of Sal – her clothes, her shoes, her jewellery, make-up, books and papers, bits and pieces.

He took himself off for a walk on the seafront but met several people who either wanted to know how she was or wanted to talk about the collision. He drove down to the nature reserve so he could walk in private but that didn't improve his mood either.

A very large G&T just made him feel maudlin. He had no appetite but by evening he decided he must eat something, so he made himself beans on toast. He opened one of his best bottles of Cotes du Rhone and worked his way steadily through it.

By ten o'clock he felt absolutely smashed and then finally the phone rang. It was Sal. She immediately knew he was drunk.

'What are you doing with yourself, other than drinking?'

'Worrying, worrying and worrying. I miss you so much Sal. I want you here. I love you Sal. Please come home.'

'We need some time apart Jim. I need to try to work stuff out in my head and you need to do the same.'

'Have you told your Mum and Dad all the gory details?'

'Mum and me have had long heart-to-hearts but I find it more difficult to talk to Dad about it. But she'll tell him.'

'I bet they think I'm a total prat.'

'Actually, Mum's very supportive of you. She thinks you've been bloody daft but she doesn't think you've been unfaithful. To be honest I'm a lot more sceptical than she is.'

'Well your Mum is one hundred percent right. I have been bloody daft, but I haven't been unfaithful. I promise you Sal, I absolutely promise you. I need you back here. Our life was so good. We've got so much together. This house is so empty, so utterly soulless without you here.'

'I love you Jim but right now I don't know if I trust you. Give the booze a rest and we'll speak tomorrow.'

He had a troubled night – half asleep and horrible senseless dreams. When he got up on Monday morning he felt disgusted with himself for hiding behind the booze. He had a determination to actually do something.

Initially he thought of jumping in the car and driving straight to Guildford to plead with Sally. Then he realised how impractical that was. She wouldn't come home with him and leave her car there and it would be messy and embarrassing for her parents to witness whatever might result.

Instead he picked the phone up and called the local florist.

'Hi Carrie, it's Jim Ellis here. Do you remember me?'

'Yes, of course Mr. Ellis. You live in my favourite house in Felixstowe. You're a good customer of mine.'

Jim gave out a forced laugh. 'Well Carrie, I need your help. My wife is at her parent's house in Guildford and I'm in the dog house.'

She laughed. 'Well it is Monday and that's 'sorry day' for florists.'

'I don't understand. What does that mean?'

'We always get orders for apology flowers on Mondays. People want to put right hiccups that happened over the weekend.'

'This was more than a hiccup Carrie.'

'So you need to send her some apology flowers. I can relay an order to a florist in Guildford for you. Tell me how much trouble you're in and I can suggest something appropriate. Usually we recommend bouquets which can cost from £25 plus delivery through to about £75.'

'Well Carrie, in that case I'd like one for £100. I'm in deep. Could you sort out one of those hand-tied bouquets in a water bubble – like I usually order for birthdays and anniversaries.'

'Certainly, we can do something really lovely for that price. What colours does she like?'

'Oh autumn colours – yellows and oranges. And can you please deliver it ASAP, I don't care what delivery costs.'

'Yes of course - and what about a card message to go with it?'

'Can I rely on your absolute discretion Carrie? It's very personal this and I wouldn't want all and sundry knowing about my problems.'

'I promise you Mr. Ellis. I'm a professional florist and it's a golden rule that we never divulge a customer's personal message to anyone other than the florist who will be making and delivering the order.'

'Okay, the message is: 'To my darling Sally. Please come home. I need you so much. With all my love Jim xxx.'

215

Carrie took the delivery address and his debit card details and wished him all the very best.

He just hoped the flowers wouldn't end up in the bin.

Chapter 28

Mary was worried about her mum. She had only moved back home the day before and had promised Mary she would keep her phone switched on and charged up.

'Brian, she's not answering. I've called both the landline and her mobile again and again but nothing. I don't like this.'

'She's probably just slept late. She's had so little sleep the past couple of weeks she must be absolutely knackered.'

'She's barely been sleeping at all since she lost Dad.'

'Maybe she had a sleeping pill and it's all caught up with her.'

'She's never taken a sleeping pill in her life. You know how she is about pills.'

'Well perhaps she's in the garden and just forgot to take the phone with her.'

'No Brian. I call her at eight every morning and she always answers. It's part of her routine.'

'Well it was part of her routine but she's got out of that routine while she's been staying with us.'

'No, it's not right. She knows how worried I was about her going home so soon.'

'Okay, if it will set your mind at rest we'll drive out there and just double check that she's okay.'

'Yeah, I'd like to – otherwise I'll be worried sick.'

The traffic from Ipswich out to Shotley was light – all the cars were travelling in the opposite direction as people headed for work.

When they pulled up outside everything looked normal. Mary had hoped to see her mum at the window. As soon as they walked up the path to her front door they knew there was something not right. There were deep scratch marks – the door had been forced.

'Mary – hold on. Let me go in first - just in case.'

But she couldn't wait. She pushed the door open and walked into the hallway, calling her mum's name. The lounge was a mess - stuff knocked over, a broken picture frame on the floor. Mary entered her mum's bedroom – she screamed and she screamed and she screamed.

Jackie Norton was lying on her back on the floor – her nightie and the carpet both absolutely soaked with blood. Mary knew she was dead. Brian knelt beside her and checked for any sign of life but he too knew there was no hope. She was cold and lifeless.

Two neighbours appeared in the room – alerted by Mary's screaming. One of them called for the police and ambulance. The dressing table drawers were open and the drawers under the bed had been pulled out. Ornaments and picture frames were scattered across the floor.

It wasn't just a murder – it was a burglary too. Mary was shaking like a leaf and crying her eyes out. She held her mum's arm and tried to cuddle her but Brian said they all should back off and not risk contaminating evidence.

A police car arrived within three minutes – it had been just up the road at the marina, on a routine patrol. A policeman and a policewoman got out. In what seemed like no time at all an ambulance arrived and then a second police car and then a third. Everyone was being ushered away from Jackie's apartment and the whole property was being taped off. A crowd was gathering despite the police telling people there was nothing to see.

Jackie Norton was confirmed dead and it wasn't long before the local press arrived. Brian confronted a journalist he knew had written about the collision and had been at Chris' funeral.

'Your bloody piece in the paper made it obvious Jackie had been staying with us in Ipswich. Some bastard must have seen it and figured this was a great opportunity to burgle an empty house.' The journalist backed off.

By mid-day the national press had arrived. There were two BBC vans, one SKY and one marked ITN. The police closed the road off. There was traffic backed up trying to leave the marina and traffic trying to get to the marina. It was obvious nobody was going anywhere.

By the early afternoon the story was on the BBC news channel and it was the lead story on the six o'clock news on both BBC and ITN and rolling news on SKY. All were giving lots of prominence to the fact that the victim had only recently survived a yachting accident which took the life of her husband.

They were all reporting the unconfirmed possibility that it had been a burglary which went wrong. The ITN reporter speculated that it was not known if the victim had confronted the burglar.

The apartment had a security system with a CCTV recording facility and the police were analysing this in the hope of finding an image of the murderer.

Colin and Saskia were sat on their balcony after a sandwich lunch. Colin was staring vacantly out to sea and Saskia was browsing on her tablet when the news flash appeared. She yelled 'oh my god, oh my god, oh my god ' and thrust her tablet at Colin before running through the lounge and into the bathroom.

He slowly took it all in but it was some time before Saskia returned – she looked as if she had been crying.

'That poor woman, that poor bloody woman. After all she's gone through – and now this.'

Colin nodded – he couldn't find any words. He was totally stunned. Saskia turned on the TV and continually switched channels to get all the different reports which were coming in.

They watched images of the Norton's house with all the emergency services in attendance and the media outside. They were re-running the news reports of the collision and of Chris Norton's funeral. The police were stonewalling and saying there would be a press briefing at 7pm. that evening.

It didn't actually take place until nearer 7.30 and they watched it on the SKY news channel. Detective Inspector John Appleton gave the briefing.

He confirmed the identity of the victim and said that at that stage they were investigating and keeping an open mind about what had happened. He did say that initial viewing of the CCTV recording did show a low-resolution image of a figure dressed all in black, wearing a dark coloured hood and gloves entering the property.

After his statement, in answer to a question from a reporter, he said that yes, it was possible that this had been a burglary which had gone wrong, but it was far too early to confirm this.

Saskia looked at Colin. 'Of course, you know what this means for you?'

He looked baffled. 'What?'

'You're off the hook. You won't be going to court.'

He didn't look pleased – he just looked puzzled.

'Are you taking this in Colin?'

'Yeah, I think so.'

'You often look like you don't know which way is up these days.'

Sally actually saw the news flash before Jim was aware of anything. She called him straight away and they both watched news coverage as they talked.

'Jim, I'm coming home in the morning. I was going to set off now but Dad says I'm in too much of a state to get on the road tonight. This is just so shocking, so totally unbelievable. I need to be with you – this is bigger than our tiff.'

221

Jim had such mixed emotions he could barely take in what was happening. The mixture of horror at what had happened to Jackie Norton, together with the relief that his wife was coming back. They talked and watched and talked and watched until they'd both seen every piece of news on every news outlet.

Steve Blake phoned his manager Andy.

'Yes Steve, I'm watching it now. That poor bloody woman. What did she do to deserve all this? It's just unbelievable – I can't take in what I'm seeing.'

'No, nor can I. This is gonna bring the collision right back into the news again.'

'It already is Steve. They're re-running all of the footage they've got from the day of the collision. I'm afraid we are centre stage again. Get ready for a lot more hassle from the media.'

'I don't want to be crass Andy but what do you think this will do to the impending court action?'

'Oh it will kill that. The person who brought the action and the key witness is dead. There won't be any court case now. It sounds awful to say this but at least Seawatch won't have to deal with all that mess.'

Mary had a tortured night – possibly the worst night of her life. In what had seemed like no time at all she had lost both her parents. Brian had fussed over her, tried to get her to eat some breakfast and said all the right things - but he kept his innermost thoughts to himself. He was wondering what Jackie had been worth and what Mary could now be worth.

Brian wandered down the garden and called Charles Walker on his mobile.

'You'll have seen the news.'

'Yes, of course. I can only offer my sincere condolences to both you and your wife. What a dreadful situation for you both.'

'Yes, it is. What will this mean for the court case?'

'Oh I'm afraid that's over. Your mother-in-law brought the case and she is the key witness in all this. There is no way it can proceed any further. I will attend to the formalities and of course there will be no liabilities for her estate. I will bear what costs had already accrued.'

'Is there no chance of me suing Colin Beaumont on my mother-in-law's behalf?'

'Oh I really wouldn't go down that path if I were you. You'd have no chance of getting a conviction. I certainly wouldn't be prepared to act on your behalf and I can't imagine any other lawyer would take it on. I'm very sorry but that's a no-brainer.'

Brian accepted that – because he had to. He worked out that with the proceeds of Jackies' house , the insurance payout for the boat and Jackie's considerable savings and investments Mary and he would come out of all this very well indeed. He couldn't be too greedy.

He had gently probed Mary about what might have been stolen from Jackie's apartment.

'Oh, most of her lovely jewellery has gone – rings, bracelets, chains and stuff. When Mum and Dad retired they bought each other really nice watches – Rolex Yacht-Masters – they're both gone. They used to keep them hidden inside a blanket in a drawer under the bed – it's as if the bastard knew where to look. They always kept a roll of cash hidden away for emergencies – that's gone too. He knew what he was doing.'

She dissolved into tears again.

It was a day of mixed emotions for both Jim and Sally. The tragedy had brought them back together. They kissed and hugged on her arrival back home. Although it was a real turning point for them they were still completely stunned and shocked by what had happened.

Over and over again they talked about the dreadful sequence of events that had seen Jackie Norton lose her husband in a terrifying collision at sea and then to lose her own life at the hands of a callous killer.

'How the hell could this have happened Jim? It's beyond coincidence. Of all the places that could have been burgled, why hers?'

'All the tabloids are linking it with the news coverage of the collision and then Chris Norton's funeral. The coverage showed both her apartment and her daughter's house and it was obvious that she'd been staying with her daughter. The assumption seems to be that some low-life had worked out that the apartment would be empty and that it was a good opportunity. Maybe when he realised she was in there he just panicked and stabbed her.'

Sally shuddered. 'I just can't take it in. It is so so awful and so dreadful that we are connected with it because of Seawatch and all that. What with the collision, the hassle Saskia has caused and two deaths it's just too much to take in.'

Jim cuddled her to him. 'We need to look after each other Sal. I've been a doughnut but let's put that behind us. I love you and I want to protect you from all the bad stuff.'

She leaned up and kissed him. 'I need you Jim – let's get our old life back.'

Chapter 29

The hooded figure parked his car and checked out the area. All was quiet and still. It was a good place to rendezvous.

He liked this client – very methodical. In fact the client had chosen the location – a small wooded area with a local road on either side. They'd agreed to park on opposite sides and then meet in a small open area in the middle. Neither of them got to see the car the other was using.

Neither of them had even seen the others face. Both dressed in dark sweat shirts and black jeans, wearing a balaclava and gloves. He thought the client really ballsy – not many people would meet a contract killer in a wood on a dark night.

The initial meeting had gone according to plan with all the details agreed and half of the money handed over in unmarked used notes. The money had been spot on – not a pound short. It was a standard agreement – half up front and half on completion.

Like him - the client had used an untraceable burner phone. This was his ninth contract and the best one – the most cautious and clued up client of them all. He still took every precaution though. He was wearing a stab vest and had a knife in his pocket.

The job had gone completely to plan. Good intelligence and also the proceeds had been a bonus. The valuables had been predictably hidden in the usual sort of places. Some online research showed the watches should raise circa 20K plus two filled pockets of nice jewellery and over a grand in cash.

He heard the client before making visual contact. Moving carefully through the wood, dressed entirely in black again. Carrying a large jiffy bag – just as with the first payment.

'All according to plan, eh?'

'Yeah, you did well. Couldn't have gone better.'

'All used notes again?'

'Yup, I've counted it three times. It's all there.'

He took the bag. 'Take care. You know how to find me if you ever need another job doing.'

'This was a one-off – and you take care too.'

They each turned and headed in opposite directions back to their cars.

Once safely back in the car, with the doors locked and the engine running, Saskia took off the balaclava. As she looked in the mirror to tidy her hair, she had a smile on her face. She thought it had been money well spent.

Also by Alan Peck

The Shotley Incident

Simon Lake was a boy seaman at HMS Ganges. When he revisits the now-derelict site over forty years later he stumbles across the dead body of a young girl.

Now the partner of a successful accountancy firm in Ipswich, Simon's world is shattered when he finds himself the prime suspect in a murder enquiry.

With the police making little progress and his life falling apart, Simon decides that it is up to him to find the killer.

Alan Peck has written various business books and for many magazines and newspapers in a career spanning the Royal Navy, IT management and retail.

As an ex-Ganges boy, now living in Ipswich, his first published novel draws upon his past experiences.

Available from Amazon at £6.99

Printed in Great Britain
by Amazon

45984900R00137